Freddy in the Fridge

Brad Herzog

Illustrated by Lydia Taranovic

Rigby

Contents

Ordinary Joe

Joe was a middle child. He lived in the middle bedroom in the middle house on a street in the middle of Middletown, Kansas. This was just about in the middle of a state that was nearly in the middle of the country. Even his last name was somewhere in the middle. Not Black. Not White. Just Gray.

Joe Gray.

Joe knew kids with names like Mario and Herman and Rashaan and Max. He had classmates who were called Billie Jean and Samantha and Amerika. He knew a Filipe. He knew a Talia. He even knew a kid named Rhythm. But Joe was just Joe.

The Gray family lived at 555 Central Avenue. Their house wasn't painted gray. It was brown with white shutters, a red door, and green trim. Of course, Joe thought, if you mix all those colors together, you'd probably get gray.

It wasn't a huge house, and it wasn't tiny. It was just crowded. Believe it or not, Joe had five older brothers and five younger brothers. Counting Joe and his mom and dad, that made 13 people in the Gray family.

Each of Joe's brothers was named after a famous person—athletes and astronauts, explorers and inventors. The oldest brother was named George. His middle name was Washington. George Washington Gray. How cool, thought Joe, to be named after the father of our country.

Joe's second oldest brother was Neil Armstrong Gray. He was named after the first man to walk on the moon. Then there was Henry Ford Gray and Paul Revere Gray and Wayne Gretzky Gray.

Then came Joe.

After Joe, his parents thought of more interesting names. VIP names. There was Christopher Columbus Gray, then Michael Jordan Gray, then the twins Orville and Wilbur Gray. They shared the same middle name—Wright. Finally, there was the baby of the family. He was tiny, just over 10 pounds, and he was all pink and cute and cuddly. His name was Arnold Palmer Gray.

Joe once asked his mother why his brothers all got fun, fancy, famous names, and he didn't. She thought for a moment and scratched her head. She fluffed up some sofa pillows and cleaned an imaginary speck of dirt off the coffee table. But she didn't have a good answer. "Ask your father," was all she said.

When Joe asked his father, he couldn't answer either. He just shrugged his shoulders. "I guess we got tired of all the fun names for a while," he said. When he saw Joe's face drop into a frown, he said, "Besides, who's to say you weren't named after the great boxer Joe Louis? Or Joe DiMaggio? Or Joe Namath? Or Joe Montana?"

But Joe checked his birth certificate. It didn't say "Montana" under "Middle Name." The only state name on there was Kansas under "Place of Birth." In fact, Joe didn't even have a middle name at all. There was no Armstrong or Jordan or Columbus. There was just a middle initial: 'B.'

Joe B. Gray.

Indeed, that pretty much describes how Joe began to feel—gray, sad, depressed. He took a look at the rest of his family, and all he saw was a bunch of stars. Each of his brothers seemed to be something special. George was the oldest, which was special enough. But he was also a hotshot lawyer in the city. Neil, the next oldest, was in college. He impressed everybody by telling them he was studying astrophysics. Joe wasn't even sure what astrophysics was. However, he was certain that a word with that many syllables must be something important. Joe didn't see George and Neil much anymore, and he missed them. But he also appreciated the extra space in the house. It meant that he had his own bedroom—even if it wasn't much bigger than the average closet. (That was the only reason he had the room, he knew. None of his older brothers wanted to live in such a small space.)

The oldest brother still living at home was Henry. He was six-foot-two and captain of the high school swim team. Paul was president of his class and a straight-A student with a sky-high IQ. And Wayne, who was 13, was known throughout town for his crazy hair. First it was spiked. Then it was bleached blonde. This week, it was part spiked and part bleached. Everybody thought Wayne was a bit odd. "He moves to the beat of a different drummer," they said. But everybody knew Wayne, and at least they heard the drumming. Joe felt like he went through life playing an invisible instrument.

Christopher was next in line among the Gray brothers—after Joe, that is. Chris was an artist. He could take almost anything—toothpicks, string, seashells, garbanzo beans—and turn it into a beautiful piece of art. Next came Michael, the musician. He was only eight, but his small hands worked magic on the black and white keys of the Gray piano.

Let's see . . . who was left? Ah, Orville and Wilbur. Well, they were twins. They looked alike. They talked alike. They walked alike. Everybody said they were "two peas in a pod" and "mirror images" and "double trouble."

"That's how you get attention," Joe said to himself. "Make sure there are two of you!" For some reason, however, Joe thought he and his twin just would have been twice as ignored.

Finally, of course, there was Arnold, the baby of the family. Everybody loves a baby. Who can resist? In fact, Arnold probably got as much attention as all the other brothers combined.

As for Joe, everything about him was average. He got average grades and was an average athlete. He wasn't tall, but he wasn't short. He wasn't thin, but he wasn't fat. He wasn't fast, but he wasn't slow. His hair wasn't dark, but it wasn't really light, either. It was just average. Joe was ordinary.

Ordinary Joe.

Around the Gray house, it was hard to get noticed. After all, there were a lot of people living there. They were slamming doors, running up the stairs, running down the stairs, talking on the phone, and surfing the Internet. They were reading books, doing homework, lounging on chairs, sharpening pencils, making sandwiches, washing dishes, and watching TV. They were blowing bubbles, running, jumping, pushing, shoving, laughing, arguing, whistling, and whining. You'd have to drive a dump truck into the living room just to get some attention.

If Joe were only old enough to drive.

Of course, everyone feels ignored sometimes. But Joe felt unusually ignored all of the time. It was almost as if he didn't exist.

For instance, his older brother Henry drove to high school every day. He would pull his old convertible out of the garage in the morning and nearly run into Joe. The brakes would squeal. The tires would screech. And Joe would make a sound that was a little bit of both.

"Sorry," Henry would say. "I didn't see you there."

It happened everywhere. Paul would come bounding down the stairs, turn a corner, and crash right into Joe. "Sorry, little buddy," he would say. "I didn't see you there."

Or Joe would be watching television in a big old chair, the kind of chair that seems to have been invented for TV watching or catnapping or fort building. Then suddenly Chris would rush into the room and jump right into Joe's lap, startling them both.

"Hey!" Joe would say.

"Whoa!" Chris would shout. "Sorry . . ."

But before his brother could finish, Joe would say, "I know. I know. You didn't see me there."

It happened in the kitchen, too. Joe would prepare his usual breakfast. He would pour some SuperCrackleFrostedFruityPops into a bowl. He'd drown the cereal in milk and set the bowl on the table. Then he would turn his back for a few seconds to grab a spoon.

When Joe would go to sit down, Wayne always seemed to be in his chair. He'd be diving into Joe's bowl of cereal with a grin on his face.

"Sorry," Wayne would say, though he clearly didn't mean it. And then he would add, "I didn't see you there."

Those same words were heard over and over again. When Michael accidentally closed the piano on Joe's fingers. When Orville flew a model airplane into Joe's toothpick sculpture. And when Wilbur did the exact same thing the very next day.

About the only time Joe felt noticed was when he would stare down at his two-month-old brother, Arnold. Arnold would look to the left, then to the right, then up, then down. Finally, he would look straight into Joe's eyes. His tiny little mouth would curl up into a great big smile.

Of course, Joe knew that at this age, it wasn't really a smile. It was just a reflex. In fact, it was probably gas. But at least Arnold wasn't saying, "Sorry, I didn't see you there." Then again, Arnold wasn't saying anything at all.

And then there were Joe's parents. He loved his mom and dad, and he knew that they loved him. They were wonderful parents. In fact, Joe believed that out of all the kids in the world, he was probably among the luckiest one percent when it came to parents. But even they were known to forget him on occasion.

Joe's father would yell loud enough so everyone in the house could hear, "Wayne! Orville! Wilbur! Everybody! Dinner's on the table!"

Or Joe's mother would shout, "Paul! Chris! Michael! Everybody! The movie starts in 10 minutes!"

Joe was always part of "Everybody." And he didn't want to be Everybody.

Joe Gray wanted to be Somebody.

Josephine, Ahab, and Sammy Purple

Tuesday was an ordinary day in the life of ordinary Joe Gray. He woke up to the sound of footsteps clomping down the hall.

Joe rolled over, trying to remember his dreams. Nothing came to mind. When it was dark, all Joe seemed to do was sleep and snore and maybe drool a little. Every morning, he'd try to recall what he had dreamed about, but he never could. It was as if someone erased his memory right before he woke up.

During the day, things were different. When it came to *day*dreaming, Joe was a lean, mean, dreaming machine. In fact, if daydreaming had been an Olympic event, he would have won more gold medals than any athlete ever. Joe could fall into a dream state at any time, in any place. And when he did, he went on spectacular adventures.

In his dreams, Joe visited stormy seas and circus tents and sold-out stadiums. Usually, these daytime mind wanderings had one thing in common: they featured Joe as the center of attention. Of course, Joe being Joe, most of the time his daydreams didn't end the way he hoped.

Joe thought about what had happened just the day before. He'd plopped himself down on a swing in the park. Of course, Joe had no intentions of merely swinging. No, he wanted to soar. He pumped as fast as he could and went as high as he could. And then . . .

He was no longer Joe B. Gray. He was Josephino, the daring young man on the flying trapeze. The Great Josephino, that is. One of the Flying Stupenda Brothers.

The Great Josephino swung from a trapeze near the top of an enormous red and white circus tent. He was 100 feet above the ground, which was swarming with circus folk of all shapes and sizes. A man walked on stilts while juggling bowling pins. Thirteen clowns climbed out of a tiny car. A trained seal balanced a beach ball on his nose. A lion tamer stuck her head inside the king of the jungle's mouth.

But all eyes were on the Great Josephino. The rest of the Flying Stupenda Brothers stood on one platform, nervously rubbing their hands together.

On another platform, the Great Josephino held a trapeze with one hand and waved to the crowd with the other.

"Please direct your attention to the top of the tent," shouted the ringmaster in Joe's head. "The Great Josephino will do a double somersault backward flip with a half-pike twist and a quadruple-turn dive."

"Ooooh!" cried the audience.

"But that's not all," added the ringmaster. "He will catch a second trapeze with his teeth!"

"Aaaah!" cried the audience.

The Great Josephino took a deep breath and then paused, just to enjoy the moment and create some anticipation for the audience.

"Remove the safety net!" Josephino shouted.

The audience gasped.

And then—away went the Great Josephino! One somersault, then another. A backward flip and a half pike. A twist, four turns, a dive, and then, the finale—

"Ooomph!" Joe said as he landed with a thud. He had been so caught up in the action that he had forgotten it was a daydream. Like the Great Josephino, Joe had let go and had flown through the air. Unlike the Great Josephino, there had been nothing there for him to catch.

So instead of grabbing a trapeze in his teeth,

Joe had ended up on his stomach in the dirt. There was no standing ovation. There was no gasp of wonder from the audience. In fact, all Joe heard was the "Caw! Caw!" of a crow. The bird—Joe's entire audience—stood on the branch of a nearby oak tree. Joe was sure the crow was laughing at him.

Now Joe rolled over in bed and rubbed the bruise on his left shin. It was a reminder that daydreaming while swinging is not a good idea.

Joe sighed, heaved himself out of bed, and headed for the shower. To his surprise, none of his brothers were there. Maybe Tuesday was going to be a better-than-average day.

As he stood there and let the water bounce off his face, Joe closed his eyes. Suddenly, he wasn't in the shower anymore. He was caught in a terrible storm in the middle of the Atlantic Ocean.

In his daydream, Joe was Captain Ahab Nemo. His floundering boat was the only hope for thousands of people on the other side of the sea. Saving thousands was a common daydream for Joe, but he liked to change the details. Sometimes, he had to save folks in England. Sometimes it was in France. Sometimes it was in the secret village of Hoobleclop in the province of Klaxwirt in the nation of Slickenbrack on the island of Flurk.

It didn't really matter whom he was saving, just that they needed to be saved. They were always threatened by a terrible disease. It could be the Blue Plague of Bellyworms or the dreaded Flummox Flu. Once in a while, it was just a really bad cold that wouldn't go away.

Actually, the disease didn't matter any more than the country did. What mattered was that Joe's ship was the only way to get the cure to its destination. The medicine came in fragile bottles and could be delivered only, for some reason, by a sailboat. (Joe didn't know why this was so. It just was.)

So Captain Ahab Nemo—otherwise known as Joe—placed his hands on the sides of the shower. He braced himself against the rocking of the waves. He shouted orders to the first mate and second mate and roommates and primates and checkmates and all the other mates on his boat. Of course, Joe had never actually been sailing, but he faked it pretty well.

"Man the jib bracket!"

"Splurf up the mainsail!"

"Reel in the flibbersquawk!"

"C'mon, boys! We can beat this storm!"

But this daydream didn't end as Joe had planned, either. He was about to sail into port. Thousands of terribly ill but wildly cheering citizens were waiting to celebrate their hero. But then, at home in Middletown, something happened. Maybe Orville flushed the downstairs toilet. Or Michael turned on the kitchen sink. Or Paul started the dishwasher.

Whatever the cause, the result was shocking. Suddenly, the warm shower of Joe's Atlantic storm slowed to a trickle—a freezing trickle! Captain Ahab Nemo was damp and shivering—and back to being just plain Joe. So much for saving thousands. So much for the hero's welcome.

Joe got out of the shower. He dried off, got dressed, combed his hair, and made goofy faces at himself in the mirror. Then, just as he opened a new tube of toothpaste, someone spoke. It was a DJ only Joe could hear.

"Ladies and gentleman," the voice said, "the greatest, coolest, handsomest . . ."

Holding the toothpaste tube like a microphone, Joe walked toward his bedroom.

" . . . the most stylish, most beloved and most famous rock star the world has ever seen . . ."

Joe nudged the bedroom door open and peeked in. He was sure he saw an audience of thousands—no, tens of thousands of people.

" . . . the King of Cool, the Maestro of Music, the Sultan of Song . . . Mister S-S-S-Sammy Purple!"

The fans screamed and waved. They shouted his name. Meanwhile, Joe/Sammy was cool, calm, and collected. He strolled to the center of the stage, where he was bathed in a white-hot spotlight. He smiled. He winked at the crowd. And then he lifted the microphone to his face and prepared to sing the first note of his new hit song.

"Crrroooooak!"

The ugly note didn't come from Joe's throat. It came from the aquarium home of his pet toad, Terrence. And it ended Joe's daydream. In fact, the croak startled Joe so much that he squeezed the tube of toothpaste. Sammy Purple the rock star was a kid again. A kid with toothpaste all over his face.

"Crrroooooak!" Terrence said again.

Joe sighed, cleaned off his face, and got dressed. Then he did the same thing he did every morning. He moped his way to the kitchen, frowned his way to the refrigerator, and opened it up.

"I'm not asking for much," he muttered as he grabbed the milk for his breakfast cereal. "Just once, I wish I could be special. Even if it's only for a day."

School Daze

*L*unch in hand, Joe headed out the door. As usual, he had a close escape with Henry and the big, ugly car he called the Henrymobile. As usual, he walked the three blocks from his house to "The Corner." That's where he always waited for the school bus.

It was sort of strange that all the kids called it "The Corner" like it was the only street corner in the area. In fact, there were exactly 43 corners in Joe's neighborhood. Joe had counted them all once. There were also 36 basketball hoops, 17 colorful banners, 9 weather vanes, 3 backyard trampolines, and a pair of plastic pink flamingos. However, "The Corner" was the only place where the school bus stopped, so it deserved some special recognition.

As Joe approached "The Corner," he could see that everyone else was already there. Suzie

O'Malley was easy to spot. She always showed up with her bright red hair in some sort of fancy hairstyle. She had names for the different styles. The Pretzel Pigtails. The Peppermint Twist. The French Fry. No one could avoid noticing Suzie.

Standing next to Suzie was her biggest rival for attention—Amerika Baines. Amerika considered herself a walking, talking fashion show. She wore clothes in colors Joe had never heard of before. Colors like aquamarine and indigo, saddle-brown and sienna, papaya-whip and peachpuff. Often, she wore three or four of these colors at the same time. Personally, Joe thought that Amerika's clothing made her look like a walking, talking fruit salad. But no one could ignore her, either.

Then there were the two other boys. The first was Herman Glick. Herman was a know-it-all who actually *did* seem to know it all. Every morning, Herman arrived complete with a new piece of trivia. Usually it was a bit of information that fell somewhere between boring and useless. For example, Herman would say, "I bet you didn't know that Arkansas and West Virginia are the only states whose names contain the names of other states." The other kids didn't know. And they didn't really care. But they always paid attention.

Next was Peter Luzinski, who usually had a

story to tell. Most of the time, it was something pretty hilarious about his Uncle Milbert, who seemed to be a few cards short of a full deck. Peter would tell about the time Uncle Milbert accidentally sat on his birthday cake. Or the time he called the bank to complain that Abe Lincoln was facing the wrong way on all the pennies. Before long, Peter would have the kids laughing so hard that their eyes bulged and their faces got red and their sides hurt.

And finally, there was Joe, who never said much at all. He usually rode the bus in silence, wishing that just once in a while the kids would pay attention to him.

Today was typical. Joe joined the group, but no one seemed to notice. They went on with their conversations as if he didn't exist.

The bus came and everyone got on. Joe took his usual seat in the middle of the bus. And, as usual, as soon as the bus started up, he began to daydream. His on-the-bus dreams were always the same. The bus was either a stagecoach bouncing through the Old West or a rocket ship blasting across the solar system. Sometimes Joe got the daydreams mixed up and had horses galloping past Jupiter or tumbleweeds bouncing through space. But today it was a stagecoach all the way.

At last the bus pulled up outside of Middletown Middle School. The brakes screeched. The door opened. Everyone piled off.

As he went down the steps, Joe looked around. At first he didn't see what he was searching for, but then he caught a glimpse of long brown hair.

The long brown hair grew on the head of Kimberly Simms, who rode a different bus. Joe had kind of known Kimberly all his life. They had been in preschool together but they had never been in the same class after that. They didn't have any classes together this year, either, but their buses let out at almost the same spot.

Joe liked Kimberly, though they hardly ever talked to each other. And when they did, their conversations were usually limited to a "hello" in front of the school. However, since this was more than most kids said to Joe, he looked forward to it.

"Hi, Joe," said Kimberly.

"Bye, Himkerly," said Joe.

Kimberly giggled, flipped her hair back over her shoulders, and started talking to Suzie and Amerika.

Joe sighed. The same thing happened every morning. He'd smile and try to say "Hi, Kimberly." But it would come out as "Ki, Himberly" or "Lie, Kimberhy" or "My,

Klimberhy" or something that sounded equally illiterate. Then she'd giggle, he'd blush, and they'd be done conversing for the day.

Head down, Joe moped his way to his first class—social studies with Mrs. Tormina. As usual, Mrs. Tormina started out with a review.

"Virginia was the first of the 13 original . . . Samantha Sherman."

Mrs. Tormina had an interesting way of teaching. She liked to give her students a chance to finish her sentences—if they raised their hands. So now Samantha Sherman called out, "Colonies!"

"Good, Samantha," said Mrs. Tormino. Then she continued, "Jefferson City is the capital of . . . Billie Jean Matheson."

Billie Jean Matheson lowered her hand and responded, "Missouri!"

Joe slumped down in his seat. He often knew the answers to Mrs. Tormina's questions. But he couldn't seem to get his hand up in time to get his name tacked on to the end of a sentence.

He wanted to. He especially wanted to give an answer that made everyone else laugh. Something like what had happened yesterday. Mrs. Tormina had said, "George Washington's wife's name was . . . Frank Buchsbaum." The whole class had erupted in laughter, including Frank Buchsbaum and Mrs. Tormina.

When he'd stopped laughing, Frank had answered, "Martha!" Then he'd added, "George never asked me to marry him." That got the whole class laughing again—even Mrs. Tormina.

More than anything, Joe wanted to make Mrs. Tormina smile with approval. Or to make the class break out in a fit of giggles. Or just to hear a line like, "The king of England during the American Revolution was . . . Joe Gray."

But as usual, Joe got through social studies without doing anything noticeable. Math was next. Joe spent the entire period trying to make sense of quadrilaterals. That is, except for when he was daydreaming about being a superhero with extrasensory powers.

Then it was time for gym. Joe had learned that this class wasn't a good time to daydream. He'd done it before and ended up with a kickball in the chest.

"Today we're going to play soccer," announced Mr. Clipowitz, the gym teacher. "Adam and Rashaan, you're the captains. Get busy and choose your teams."

Of course, Joe was never a captain. And he was never one of the first players picked—or one of the last. Just like everything else in his life, he was always somewhere in the middle. So it was no surprise when his name was called halfway through the process of team selection.

The game started with everyone doing what they did best. Rashaan James, the best passer, kicked the ball toward Adam Hanson. Adam, who was the best kicker, boomed the ball toward the goal. And Max Kline, who was the best goalie, made a great save.

Joe was best at being ignored. So he stood on the left side of the gym. He knew the ball would never come his way.

Joe wished he could take control of the ball with a bit of fancy footwork. He would have been thrilled if he could dribble the ball the length of the field while the other kids shouted with pleasure (his teammates) or panic (his opponents). He would have jumped for joy if he could boom a high kick into the top left corner of the net.

But nothing like this had ever happened—or was likely to happen. Sometimes, Joe would go the whole gym class without once touching the ball. It was as if he was invisible. The Invisible Soccer Player.

Despite his determination not to daydream during gym, Joe's imagination took over. He *was* the Invisible Soccer Player—the hero of his team.

And the semifinals of the season were at hand.

"Whoa! Where's the ball going?" said Max (in Joe's daydream).

"But that's impossible!" shouted Adam. "There's nobody near it!"

"I know who it is!" said Rashaan. "It's that superstar sportsman, that phantom of fancy footwork, that ghostly game player—the Invisible Soccer Player. Nobody can stop him!"

The Invisible Soccer Player sped toward the opposing goalie, who was waiting in terror. He planted his invisible left foot in the turf, drew back his invisible right foot, and blasted the ball with his powerful and invisible toes.

"Ooomph!" said Joe.

The daydream was over. A soccer ball had landed right in his not-so-invisible stomach.

"Pay attention!" shouted Max and Adam and Rashaan and Mr. Clipowitz.

And all Joe could think was, why don't they pay attention to me?

After gym class came Joe's favorite time of day—lunch. The lunchroom at Middletown Middle School was a fun place, mostly because the kids had created an interesting game to play. They called it the Super Sandwich Taste-Off. Each day, three or four kids would open their brown lunch bags or their lunch boxes or their lunch containers. (One kid even had a lunch bucket). Then they'd pull out special sandwiches they had made themselves.

These sandwiches could be scrumptious or surprising or even a little strange. There were combinations like peanut butter and pickles on pumpernickel. Or meatloaf and mustard on whole wheat. Or liverwurst and lime juice on French bread. The most famous sandwich so far had been brought in by Tommy Terwilliger. It had consisted of corned beef, cucumbers, coconut, cream cheese, and ketchup on a Kaiser roll.

A group of seven kids who called themselves the Sandwich Board tasted all of the sandwiches entered in each day's Taste-Off. Then they decided which one they liked the best. Talk about attention! Winning the Super Sandwich Taste-Off was like winning the Super Bowl—the World Series—the lottery!

Or so Joe figured. He had never been involved. With so many hungry boys in his house, there was never enough food left over for Joe to make a goofy sandwich. Besides, he didn't have the courage to enter the Taste-Off.

So now other kids opened their lunches to find roast beef and relish on rye or salami and sauerkraut on sourdough. Joe pulled out two pieces of white bread with a slice of bologna stuck in between.

Nobody is going to notice this sandwich, he thought.

Nobody did.

After lunch, Joe moped through the afternoon, looking forward to the end of the day. His last class was science with Mr. Berg.

Mr. Berg looked exactly the way Joe imagined a mad scientist would look. He wore a long white coat and carried a clipboard. Nobody ever saw him use the pockets of his coat, except as a place to hold a fancy fountain pen. And nobody ever saw him use the fountain pen to write anything on his clipboard. Nobody ever saw Mr. Berg comb his hair, either. He had white hair that stuck out in every direction. It looked like Mr. Berg prepared for school every morning by sticking his finger in a light socket.

"Today we are going to do some experiments with chemicals," Mr. Berg said.

Joe perked up. This sounded interesting.

"Tommy Terwilliger, you're first," said Mr. Berg.

Tommy went to the front of the room. While Mr. Berg directed him, Tommy mixed two different chemicals in a test tube. At once a pink, bubbly foam erupted over the sides. Everyone oohed and aahed.

Juan Lugo was next. He combined a clear liquid and a white one. To everyone's surprise, he ended up with something milky-green.

Then it was Max Kline's turn. He mixed his two chemicals and suddenly there was a dull "poof" from the test tube. A mini-explosion!

"Joe Gray, you can conduct the next experiment," Mr. Berg said.

Joe made his way to the front of the room. His heart beat rapidly. What exciting combination would he make, he wondered.

"Mix these two chemicals," instructed Mr. Berg. He handed Joe two containers, each holding a clear liquid.

Joe poured a little of the first chemical into the test tube. Then a little of the second.

What did he get? A clear liquid.

"You see, class. Not every mix of chemicals produces a noticeable reaction," said Mr. Berg.

"Figures," Joe muttered.

Meet Freddy

Wednesday was a extraordinary day. A day that changed Joe's life. But before that fateful day could begin, there was a fateful night.

In the beginning, it seemed to be a night like all other nights. Joe slept. Joe snored. Joe drooled a little. Joe didn't dream. But as the darkness of night evolved into the dim light of early morning, Joe suddenly sat up in bed. He was sure something had brushed against his cheek or scratched his wrist or mussed his hair. Or maybe all three at once.

Whatever it was that had happened, he was awake now. And, even though it was much earlier than his normal breakfast time, he was unusually hungry.

Joe hopped out of his bed in the middle of his bedroom in the middle of the hall. There's nothing wrong with a little midnight snack, he thought. Even if it is actually 5:23 in the morning.

Half asleep, Joe shuffled down the hall, down the stairs, and through the living room. As he did, he started to feel the way he felt when he was wide awake—gray, sad, depressed. So Joe fell into his old routine. He moped his way to the kitchen, frowned his way to the refrigerator, and glumly opened it up.

"Just once," Joe said, as he searched for a slice of cheese, "I wish I could be—"

"Special?" interrupted a voice from inside the refrigerator. "Then why don't you do something about it?"

"What? Who? Huh?" asked Joe.

"I said, 'Why don't you do something about it?'" It was an odd voice—somehow gruff and squeaky at the same time.

Joe jumped back. He looked to the left. He looked to the right. Finally, he peered back into the fridge. He checked the exact spot that the voice seemed to come from. It was a container of cottage cheese. The last time Joe had checked, cottage cheese couldn't talk.

"I must be losing my marbles," Joe said to himself, as he reached for the container.

"Well, you certainly won't find them in the refrigerator," replied the voice.

This time, Joe didn't jump backward. He leaped two feet into the air. He banged his head against the freezer door and fell to the kitchen floor. The container of cottage cheese did one somersault, then another, then a flip. It continued with a half-pike, a twist, a turn, another turn, and a third turn. Then—plop!—the cottage cheese landed upside down on Joe's chest.

"It looks like I have my work cut out for me," said the voice.

Joe was sure he was dreaming. He looked up to see a tiny man step from behind a bottle of Thousand Island dressing. The man couldn't have been more than 8 inches tall. He wore a bright orange top hat, a lime green jacket, and boots as yellow as ripe bananas. But the strangest thing—besides the fact that he was an 8-inch-tall man who was living in Joe's refrigerator—was his beard. It was pale purple, the color of a lilac bush.

Joe was practically speechless. "What? Who? Huh?" was all he could say.

"Allow me to introduce myself," said the miniature man. "I'm Frederick Engelbert Ichabod Hortense Ezekiel Jebidiah Plotzkriggle the Fifth." He pulled off his top hat and bowed politely. "But you can call me Freddy."

"Freddy?" echoed Joe.

"Freddy."

31

Joe wasn't sure if he was startled or stunned or flabbergasted—or dreaming. He pinched himself to be sure.

"Ouch," he said.

"See," said the tiny man with the pale purple beard, "you're wide awake."

"But how . . . what . . . who are you?" asked Joe.

"You mean you've never heard about the little man who turns the light off every time you close the refrigerator?"

"Sure, but—"

"Your older brothers didn't believe in me," said Freddy. He shook his head as if it were completely reasonable that a mini-man was living next to the leftover chicken drumsticks. He sat on a wrapped package of butter and let his legs dangle over the side.

"They tried every method they could to find out if and how the light in the fridge actually turned off," Freddy continued. "First there was George. He thought he was clever. His idea was to attach a thermometer to the light bulb in the fridge. Then he left the refrigerator door shut for ten minutes. When he reopened it, he checked the thermometer. He figured if it was still cold inside, that would prove that the bulb was off when the door was closed. But I outsmarted George."

"What did you do?" asked Joe, who was surprised at how calm he was. After all, he was talking to a man the size of a cucumber.

"Every time George opened the door," Freddy grinned, "he found that the thermometer had 'fallen' into the cottage cheese."

Freddy started pacing back and forth on the stick of butter. "Next came Neil. He tried to use a camera with a self-timer. Very ingenious."

"And?" asked Joe.

"And I took it upon myself to turn the camera's flash on. So Neil thought the fridge light was on, but it was really the flash bulb. You have to be more clever than that if you're going to outwit Frederick Plotzkriggle the Fifth."

Freddy leaped off the butter onto the top of a plastic container of sliced cantaloupe. "Henry was next. He tried much the same thing, only with a camcorder. He figured he would rewind the tape to see if the light was on or off when the door was closed. But all I had to do was turn the camcorder from "record" to "play" every time. Boy, was he frustrated!" said Freddy, beaming with pride.

"And Paul?"

"Let's see," said Freddy, as he lifted his orange top hat and scratched the top of his tiny head. "Paul was the high-tech one. What do you call it, a webcam? He installed one in the refrigerator and expected to watch what happened on the Internet."

"So how did you take care of that?" Joe asked.

"Easy," said Freddy. "Do you know what happens when you spill a little milk on a webcam? Pzzzzzttttt!" Freddy laughed so hard he nearly fell into a half-open container of rice pudding.

Joe struggled not to laugh. It *was* kind of funny to think about his older brothers being outsmarted. Especially by a man who wore a hat the size of a thimble. But wait a minute—

"What about Wayne?" Joe asked. "Didn't he try?"

Freddy shrugged. "That Wayne isn't the brightest fellow, is he? He just opens the door, sticks his head in the refrigerator, grabs whatever's closest, and shuts the door again. Open and shut, open and shut, open and shut. All he cares about is that there's food inside. That boy can eat!"

"So tell me," said Joe. "*Do* you turn the light off every time we close the refrigerator door?"

Joe really wanted to know. After all, wasn't this one of life's great questions? To Joe, the list looked sort of like this:

1. Why am I here?
2. Where does the universe end?

3. Is there intelligent life on other planets?

4. Does the refrigerator light go out when you close the door?

Freddy smiled and answered Joe's question with another question. "If a tree falls in the woods, but nobody is there to hear it, but somebody left a tape recorder there, but the tape recorder is on the fritz, but somebody comes along to fix the tape recorder and shouts something into it just as the tree falls, does the tree actually make a sound?"

Freddy crossed his arms and looked as if he had just said something truly brilliant.

"I . . . I really don't know," Joe replied.

"That's my point," said Freddy.

"Uh, okay." Joe wasn't sure if he was confused or bewildered or totally befuddled. He was beginning to feel that understanding Freddy might require a decoder ring.

"So, uh, Freddy, why are you talking to me? I'm nobody."

Freddy stood up to his full 8-inch height and pointed a minuscule finger in Joe's face. "First of all, you're *not* nobody," he nearly shouted, in that gruff-squeaky sort of way. "If you were nobody, how could we be having this conversation? I'd be talking to myself right now. And I'm clearly not talking to myself because if I were, I wouldn't have to shout. In fact, I wouldn't even have to whisper. You can talk to yourself without even talking. You just have to think to yourself. But I'm not thinking. I'm talking. Got it?"

"Well . . ."

"Now, you're not nobody, but you're not everybody, either. If you were everybody, how could you possibly fit in your kitchen? Everybody amounts to several billion people. And that doesn't even include all the hyenas, giraffes, sea cows, and ladybugs. Personally, I've never seen a giraffe open a refrigerator. So that doesn't make any sense at all."

"Ummm . . ."

"So you're not nobody and you're not everybody," said Freddy. "That means you must be somebody."

"I'm somebody?" asked Joe, who had always wanted to be just that.

"You're somebody," said Freddy.

Joe gave up. "Okay, I'm somebody. But why are you talking to me? Why this particular somebody?"

"Two reasons," said Freddy, as he reached into his lime green jacket. "The first one is this . . . ." He pulled out a paper scroll and unrolled it. The paper was longer than he was tall. "I have a list of concerns about the state of your refrigerator. I demand that you communicate my complaints to your parents."

"Complaints? But . . . "

Too late. Freddy began reciting from the list. "You have a half cup of lima beans that have been sitting in the back of the second shelf since July. You have a can of tomato paste in the corner of the bottom shelf that has been there so long you could make bricks out of it. You have some cheddar cheese that has so much mold that it's turned green. And does anyone in your house actually eat mangoes? Apparently not. That jar of sliced mangoes has been in here almost as long as I have."

"Okay . . ."

"Now, take a look at the yogurt container," Freddy continued. "See the date on the bottom? Your mom bought that 6 months ago. Are you going to tell me that whatever's inside is still going to look like yogurt? I don't think so. I dare you to open it. Really, I dare you."

"No thanks. I'll take your word for it," said Joe. He was secretly thankful for the information, since he had been considering eating that yogurt.

"And finally," announced Freddy, "see that bag toward the back of the third shelf? Last November, your dad put a couple of pieces of chicken in there. He was planning to make chicken stock. You know, for soup. He actually came close to doing it one day, but then he realized he didn't have any onions. Everybody knows you need onions if you're going to make chicken stock. He said he was going to make a trip to the grocery store for some onions, but he never did. Well, to make a long story short, we're coming up on November again. Don't you think it's time to get rid of the chicken?"

Freddy did a perfect back flip and landed softly on a loaf of bread. "After all," he said, "how would you like it if you had to sleep next to rotten chicken, lumpy yogurt, crusty tomato paste, and moldy cheese?"

Joe had to admit the idea didn't sound appealing. "Okay, I promise we'll clean up our . . . I mean, your fridge." Then he stuck his head halfway into the refrigerator and looked Freddy straight in the eyes. "So what's the second reason you're talking to me?"

Freddy looked right back at him. "I've decided to help you."

"Help me?"

"Help you."

"Help me how?" asked Joe.

"Well, every day lately you've been opening the refrigerator door and making a wish. You know the wish I'm talking about. You didn't know it at the time, but each time you made that wish you were looking at me."

"But I couldn't see you," said Joe.

"I only allow myself to be seen when I want to be seen," said Freddy. "And that has happened exactly, let's see . . ." He began to count on his fingers, " . . . never."

"Never?"

"Never."

"So none of my brothers has met you?"

"Nope. In fact, as far as I know, very few people ever get to meet one of the famous little men in the fridge." Freddy grinned. "I guess that would make you rather special now, wouldn't it?"

Joe stood up straight, raised an eyebrow, and allowed a slight smile to appear. "Gee, I guess it would."

Going Bananas

"So let me get this straight," said Joe. He was preparing a heaping bowl of SuperCrackle-FrostedFruityPops while Freddy sat on his shoulder. "I can see you, but nobody else can?"

"Right."

"And I can hear you, but nobody else can?"

"Not exactly," said Freddy. "Other people can hear me. But only if I throw my voice and make it sound like yours."

"Huh?"

"Like a ventriloquist," Freddy explained. "Not that I'm saying you're a dummy."

"Very funny," said Joe. "Now let me get this straight. Other people can't see you. And they can only hear you if you sound exactly like me. So how am I supposed to show you off to all the kids?"

"Ay, there's the rub," said Freddy.

Joe wasn't exactly sure what that meant.

However, he remembered hearing it recently on a TV show. Maybe that's where Freddy had picked it up—when Henry or Michael or Paul or someone had opened the fridge to get a TV-time snack.

At any rate, Joe was impressed because he had always wanted to use the phrase himself. He figured it made as much sense as most of what he'd heard on television. Things like "What's up, Doc?," "Yabba-dabba-do," and "Is that your final answer?"

Freddy leaped off Joe's shoulder, bounced off a sponge next to the kitchen sink, and landed in an empty teacup.

"So, Joe," he said, "what you're worried about is that no one will believe you, right?"

Joe shrugged. "I guess," he said.

"What if told you that I play cards every Wednesday night with Santa Claus, the Easter Bunny, and the Tooth Fairy. Would you believe me?"

Joe was pouring milk into his bowl. He almost spilled it because he laughed so hard. "Probably not," he said when he could talk.

"Well, I do. And between you and me, that Tooth Fairy is a terrible cheater."

"I find all this a bit hard to believe," said Joe. Of course, he also found it hard to believe that he was talking to a tiny bearded fellow sitting in a teacup.

"That's my point. It's true, but there's no way I can prove it. And the more I talk about it, the more you might think I have rocks in my head or bats in my belfry."

Uh-oh, thought Joe. He already knew that once Freddy got going, it was hard to stop him.

"Or I've flipped my lid or I'm a few bricks shy of a load."

"I understand," interrupted Joe.

"I'm not done yet," said Freddy. "My favorites are the food ones. I could be nutty as a fruitcake. Or maybe I've gone bananas—which reminds me, I'll be right back."

With that, Freddy pulled a banana out of his lime green jacket. How he did it, Joe had no idea. After all, the banana was as big as Freddy.

Holding the banana under his arm like a football, Freddy hopped off the kitchen counter. He made a soft landing on Joe's shoe and ran out the front door. He was back inside two minutes later.

"What did you just do?" asked Joe.

"You'll find out soon," Freddy replied. "Now where were we?"

"You were as nutty as a fruitcake, I think."

"Oh, right. So I was."

"And you're saying everyone will think I'm as nutty as a fruitcake, too. At least they will if I go around telling them I've got a new friend. Someone they can't see or hear, but who happens to be one of the little men who turns the light off in the fridge."

"Exactly," Freddy nodded, "although I've never actually told you whether I turn the light off or not."

Joe frowned. "Well then, how am I supposed to get noticed? I mean, knowing you is the most noticeable thing about me. And nobody can notice you."

"There are many ways of getting noticed," said Freddy with a wink. "Just leave it to me. And now, it's time to get to work."

In the blink of an eye, Freddy reached into his jacket and pulled out a salt shaker. Again, Joe couldn't figure out how the little man could fit something that large into a jacket the size of a small lime. But he was more interested in what Freddy was going to do with the salt than in where it came from.

Freddy jumped up on the counter next to Joe's cereal bowl. With a great heave, he upended the shaker over the edge of the bowl.

"Hey!" cried Joe. "What are you doing?"

"Relax," said Freddie. "It's not like you ever get

to eat the cereal you've fixed. Now take this and put it on the table."

"First tell me what you're up to."

"Just do it," said Freddy, sounding very forceful.

Sounding forceful was quite an accomplishment for someone with a head the size of a walnut and a voice that sounded like a mouse with laryngitis. So Joe followed orders.

"There, the cereal's on the table. Now what?" Joe asked.

Freddy checked a teensy-weensy watch on his itsy-bitsy wrist. "Any second now," he said.

Indeed, a moment later, Wayne rushed into the room.

"Pretend you don't see him," whispered Freddy.

Joe shrugged and turned his back to the kitchen table. When he turned around a moment later, Wayne was sitting in front of the bowl of cereal. He had Joe's spoon in his hand and a grin on his face. He took a big spoonful of SuperCrackleFrostedFruityPops. As he lifted the spoon to his mouth, Wayne said, "Sorry, I didn't see you there."

Then he shoved the spoon in his mouth and swallowed.

"Ugggh!"

Cereal and milk sprayed across the table. Wayne jumped up, knocking the chair over. He dashed to the sink, turned on the faucet, and stuck his open mouth underneath.

Then Freddy completed his trick. As Wayne raised his dripping face from the sink, the little man threw his voice. So it sounded like Joe was talking when someone said, "Well, do you see me *now?*"

Joe felt that Wayne had gotten what he deserved. Still, he was a little shocked. What have I gotten myself into? he wondered.

However, he only had a few seconds to wonder. Because when he saw the look on Wayne's face, Joe knew exactly what to do—run!

He ran through the TV room, through the living room, through the dining room, and to the bottom of the stairs. There he paused to listen for Wayne coming in pursuit. At the same time, Freddy, who had been clinging to Joe's shoulder, put a hand behind one tiny ear. He was listening for something, too.

"Right on time," Freddy said with a grin. This only confused Joe. Then Freddy pulled a cream-filled donut from his jacket. "Here, hold this," he said.

As Joe reached for the donut, Freddy threw himself against its sugary side.

Splat!

Freddy had remembered what Joe had forgotten. This was the time every morning when Paul came bounding down the stairs. The time when he would knock over his brother on the way. And then he'd say, "Sorry, little brother. I didn't see you there."

But today, Paul got a surprise. He got a face

full of creamy filling.

Again, Freddy threw his voice. "Do you see me *now?*" he asked, sounding just like Joe.

And again, Joe knew exactly what to do—run. He grabbed his lunch bag and his backpack. Then he dashed outside, with Freddy clinging to his shoulder.

As he reached the driveway, Joe remembered what usually came next—at least on ordinary mornings—he would encounter yet another brother who wouldn't notice him. It would be Henry, driving the Henrymobile.

Joe braced for the squeal of brakes and the screech of tires. Instead, he heard a ker-thickety-thickety. Then another ker-thickety-thickety. Followed by a ker-rrrr-rrrr, a pffffff, and finally, a ssssss-clack.

Joe decided to keep running. He glanced over his shoulder to see Henry angrily step out of the driver's seat and walk to the back of his car. Was that a banana stuck in the tailpipe?

Waving the banana angrily, Henry took off after Joe. He was closely followed by Wayne, who was still dripping wet. And then by Paul, who was still wiping creamy filling from his face.

Anyone who has brothers knows how Joe felt. It's scary to be chased by one older brother. Being chased by two can only be described as terrifying. As for being chased by *three* older brothers, well, Joe had never run faster in his life.

"It wasn't me!" Joe yelled over his shoulder. (The other shoulder, that is. The one that wasn't holding a little bearded man.)

Joe ran through Mrs. Fishbein's backyard. He jumped over Mr. and Mrs. Pinsky's hedges. He ducked under Mr. Pichetti's volleyball net. He ran and ran and ran until finally he realized his brothers weren't chasing him anymore.

"What . . . in the world . . . are you trying . . . to do . . . to me?" Joe gasped.

"You felt like you weren't being noticed," said Freddy. "It's my mission to fix that."

"Well . . . it's one thing . . . to get attention," Joe wheezed. "It's another thing . . . to become . . . a moving target."

"Don't you worry," said Freddy, tipping his little orange top hat. "I have all kinds of plans."

As they made their way toward the bus stop, Joe wondered and worried. It seemed like the little man from the fridge was cooking up a recipe for trouble.

6

Terrence's Wild Ride

"**M**y Uncle Milbert stopped by yesterday," said Peter Luzinski as the school bus rumbled through the heart of Middletown. The other kids flashed grins at each other. They just knew there was a good story coming.

"He wanted to drop off a card for my sister," Peter continued.

"Was it her birthday?" someone asked.

"Nope. It was her half birthday."

"Her half birthday?" asked that same someone.

"Uh-huh. Uncle Milbert thinks birthdays are a dime a dozen. Everybody celebrates them, so they're not a big deal anymore. A few years ago, he decided to start celebrating people's half birthdays. He figured nobody celebrates those, so the occasion would be special."

"How do you celebrate a half birthday?" asked another listener.

"Well, usually he stops by at half past the hour," Peter explained. "Sometimes he bakes half a cake and he places, say, ten and a half candles on top of it. Once in a while, he surprises us with what he calls a half-gift. He'll give us a half-dollar or a photograph of a flag at half-mast or a cookie shaped like a half-moon. Once he even celebrated my cousin Leo's half birthday by teaching him a wrestling move called the half nelson. My dad says half birthdays are a half-baked idea, but that's just Uncle Milbert."

Peter looked around and saw that he had the attention of half the kids on the bus. "Anyway, back to my story. Uncle Milbert stopped by with a card for my sister."

"Why didn't he mail it?" asked somebody a few seats behind Peter.

"That's what my dad asked him. First Uncle Milbert said he did it to save money. But Dad pointed out that the gas he used to get to our house probably cost more than a stamp would. So then Uncle Milbert said it was because he doesn't trust the post office anymore."

"Why not?" someone asked.

"Because of an experiment he did last week," said Peter. "Uncle Milbert says he decided to test the post office. So he put a dollar bill in an envelope and mailed it to himself. The envelope arrived and there was a dollar bill inside. But Uncle Milbert says it was a different dollar bill—not the one he put in there."

"That's ridiculous," said half the listeners. The other half just shook their heads.

"That's Uncle Milbert," said Peter. "He's a strange one, I tell ya."

The kids laughed at another well-told Peter Luzinski story. Even Joe couldn't help but smile.

Freddy was still seated on Joe's shoulder. But the little man wasn't watching Peter or the other kids. He was watching Joe.

"Next time," said Peter, "I'll have to tell you all about the time Uncle Milbert met the president."

"The president?" repeated a couple of kids. "The president of the United States?"

"Yep, on the golf course," Peter smiled. "The leader of the free world conked Uncle Milbert on the head with a golf ball. Come to think of it, that might explain a lot of things."

When the laughter died down, Herman Glick decided it was time for him to take center stage. "I bet you didn't know this," he said, as he rubbed his eyeglasses on his shirt. "The most common first name for U.S. presidents is James."

He was talking to nobody in particular, and

nobody in particular was listening. But although they'd never admit it, the kids found this useless trivia somewhat interesting. So they each listened with one ear.

"Yep, that's right," Herman continued. "There have been four presidents named William and four named John. But I can come up with six named James. Can you?"

The question was met by several seconds of silence. This was usually the case when the resident Know-It-All tried to Show-Off-It-All on the bus. But then some of the kids began to chime in for fun.

"*James and the Giant Peach,*" said one, and everyone smiled and snickered.

"Jim Henson," said another, and the rest of the bus chortled and giggled.

"Jiminy Cricket," said a third, and everyone guffawed and slapped their knees.

"Gym shoes!" shouted a voice that sounded just like Joe's. Except that it couldn't have been, because Joe hadn't said anything.

There was a split second of silence. Then the other kids roared and whooped with laughter. They winked at Joe. They grinned at him.

And Joe beamed with pride, happy to be the center of attention. The little purple-bearded ventriloquist sitting on his shoulder beamed, too.

"Very funny. No, really," said Herman. "There was James Madison and James Monroe and James Polk and James Buchanan and James Garfield. The last one was James Carter, but everyone called him Jimmy."

There was a collective "Hmmm" from the kids on the bus. It was a well-rehearsed reaction. One that made them sound half interested and half bored at the same time.

"Of course," Herman continued, "there have also been presidents named Millard, Ulysses, Lyndon, Woodrow, Grover . . . ."

This got the kids laughing again. Mostly because they immediately pictured Grover of Sesame Street fame sitting behind a big desk in the Oval Office.

"Who was his vice president?" asked that Joe-like voice. "Elmo?"

Again, the kids nearly fell out of their seats laughing. Joe tried to give Freddy an angry look, but he couldn't quite pull it off. He was too happy about being noticed to be mad.

When the laughter died down, Herman turned to Suzie O'Malley. "Hey, nice hairdo," he said.

Everyone looked at Suzie. Once again she had tied her bright red hair into knots and braids. It was a hairdo that had never before been seen on a Middletown Middle School student.

Suzie pretended to be embarrassed by the attention, even though she clearly loved it. "Yes," she said, sounding like an actress in a soap opera who was accepting an award. "It's a new style I'm trying. I haven't quite figured out what to call it."

Several kids examined the loops and twists in her hair and tried to come up with a suitable name.

"How about the Y Knot?" suggested Peter. Suzie made a face to show her displeasure.

"The Triple Flip," said Herman, which caused Suzie to frown.

"The Kansas Crown," said Amerika. Suzie shook her head.

"How about the Suzie Q?" asked Freddy, pretending he was Joe.

Suzie perked up. "Hey, that's not bad," she admitted. "The Suzie Q . . . Suzie Q . . . I like it," she said to Joe. "Thanks."

Joe beamed again. This new, witty Joe Gray was a pretty popular guy. And it was all thanks to the tiny man sitting on his shoulder.

"So what do you think of my outfit?" Amerika Baines asked.

Without waiting for a reply, she went on to

describe the colors of the day. "My T-shirt is cornflower blue. This vest is medium spring green with cream-colored pockets. The fringe at the bottom of my pants is goldenrod. My boots may look pinkish, but the color is actually called salmon. And my hat isn't yellow. It's lemon chiffon."

"Cool," said Peter.

"Colorful," said Suzie.

"Creative," said Herman.

"What about you, Joe?" Amerika asked. "What do you think?"

This time, everyone looked straight at Joe, which was an uncommon experience for him. Freddy, still invisible next to him, couldn't possibly throw his voice again. Everyone would notice that Joe's lips hadn't moved.

So Freddy left it up to Joe to sound like Joe. "C'mon, tell her what you think," the purple-bearded mini-man whispered.

"Hmmm," Joe said, as he took in Amerika's colorful outfit. "It sort of looks like you got too close to a crayon box that exploded."

Joe expected another laugh. After all, he had been cracking the kids up for several miles now. Well, at least his voice had been cracking them up, even if it had been telling Freddy's jokes.

But this time there was total silence. Peter looked at Herman. Herman looked at Suzie. Suzie looked at Amerika. Amerika looked upset.

"That wasn't a very nice thing to say," Amerika said. The murmurs from the rest of the kids indicated they agreed wholeheartedly.

Then Amerika got even. "You're just jealous, Joe. After all, there's nothing special about the way *you* dress. Faded old blue jeans. An ugly gray shirt. A dirty gray hat. I don't see anything special at all."

Joe's face fell. His shoulders slumped. His heart dropped to his sneakers. Those were exactly the words he didn't want to hear.

Then Freddy spoke into Joe's left ear. "Take off your hat," the little man said.

"What?" Joe was talking to Freddy, but Amerika thought he was talking to her.

"I said that I don't see anything special about you," she repeated.

Meanwhile, Freddy said again, 'Take off your hat. I put something special under there."

As usual, Joe wore a baseball cap. This one was gray one with a red "B" on the front. His dad had told him it was an old Brooklyn Dodgers baseball cap that he bought at the Baseball Hall of Fame. However, Joe preferred to think of the "B" as a declaration of his middle name. In his imagination, the "B" in Joe B. Gray and the "B" on his hat stood for something interesting like Bartholomew or Buddy or Boris or Belvedere.

Joe had been thinking that his head felt a bit odd. But with all the commotion this morning, he hadn't really investigated the matter. Now he gave Freddy a curious look and then slowly removed the cap.

"Crrrooooooak!"

It was Terrence. The toad was sitting atop Joe's head like a king on a throne. A smelly, sticky king with bumpy warts and bulbous eyes.

Amerika yelped in surprise. So did Suzie and

Peter. Herman jumped backward in shock. If he could have fit through the bus window, he would have.

Before Joe could grab the toad, it took a flying leap—and landed right in Amerika's lap.

Amerika screamed again, this time much louder. The sound made Terrence jump again. He landed right on the frame of Herman's glasses.

When Herman went to grab the toad, Terrence took off. With one great leap, he went over Peter's head and into Suzie's hair.

Suzie started yelling and beating her hands at her head. By the time she managed to free Terrence from her famous red locks, she no longer had a Suzie Q hairstyle. She had more of a hair-after-a-hurricane style.

So Suzie was screeching, Amerika was screaming, Peter was yelling, and Herman was wheezing. The whole bus had erupted in pandemonium.

The bus screeched to a halt. Ozzie, the driver, slowly rose from his seat. Eyes blazing, he headed for the middle of the bus.

"What is going on here?" Ozzie asked in measured tones.

Everyone explained at once. Everyone but Joe, that is.

In a matter of moments, Terrence was in

custody. So was Joe. He was sitting in the "trouble seat"—the one right behind the driver. The one where anyone who caused problems had to sit.

When they got to school, Ozzie escorted both Terrence and Joe off the bus. They walked right past Kimberly Simms, who offered her usual "Hi, Joe."

But Joe had no time to say "Ki, Himberly," or "Bye, Himkerly," or "My, Klimberhy."

He was on his way to the principal's office.

Off to the Office

Joe fidgeted in the uncomfortable chair. On any other occasion, the chair probably would have been fine. But when a boy is waiting to see the principal because he's in trouble, there's no comfort to be found.

Joe wasn't sure what to do with himself while he waited. He wiped an imaginary speck of dirt off his shirt. He rubbed an imaginary stain off the table. He stared at an imaginary spot on the wall. Finally, he began to wonder if Freddy was actually a figment of his imagination, too. A little man who lives in a refrigerator? It was ridiculous . . . preposterous . . . ludicrous!

"Adventurous, aren't I?" said a voice that came out of nowhere. That voice that was both squeaky and gruff. That voice that could belong only to Freddy.

"Oh no," moaned Joe.

Just then the tiny man popped into view. He did a cartwheel across the coffee table and landed with a miniature thud on a chair across from Joe.

"Hello, Joe Gray," Freddy said. "I bet you're starting to feel special now."

"Special?" echoed Joe. "Special? I'm waiting to be called into the principal's office. That's not special. That's trouble."

Freddy smiled. "Ah," he said, "but how many other kids in your class are going to be called to the principal's office today?"

Joe frowned. "Probably nobody."

"Well, my dictionary defines 'special' as . . . let's see . . ."

Somehow Freddy managed to pull a full-size dictionary out of his tiny jacket. "Yes, here it is. 'Special: distinguished by some unusual quality; unique.'"

"So?" replied Joe. He was still trying to figure out where the dictionary came from. He could only guess that Terrence was croaking somewhere inside Freddy's jacket, too.

"So you're officially special," said Freddy with a grin.

"Well, this isn't the kind of special I wanted," said Joe, rubbing his forehead.

"Now, don't get picky on me."

"Picky? You brought a toad onto the school bus! You got me sent to the principal's office for the first time ever! I've known you for just a couple hours, and you've already made my life—"

"Not boring." Freddy finished the sentence for Joe.

"Arrrggghh!" was all Joe could say. He threw his hands into the air. Meanwhile, Freddy flipped through the dictionary again.

"You know," said the man from the fridge, "this dictionary defines 'refrigerate' as 'to cool or chill.'"

"So?" said Joe.

"So be cool. Chill out," Freddy suggested. "I promise you this: I'll put a smile back on your face in no time."

Joe found that hard to believe. He wasn't sure he'd ever smile again. He closed his eyes, hoping that when he opened them, Freddy might have disappeared.

A few seconds later, he heard a low voice say, "Wake up, Joe Gray!"

Joe's eyes snapped open. A tall man with bushy eyebrows and dark eyes stood in front of him. It was Mr. Trevor, the principal.

Joe gulped. He didn't know exactly what went on when a kid got sent to the principal's office. He knew it had happened to his brothers often enough. But they had never seemed to want to talk about the experience at the dinner table.

Now Joe's imagination filled in the blanks. Maybe Mr. Trevor had one of those wooden stocks like the Pilgrims had used. The things in which your hands and head were locked up until someone decided you had been punished enough.

Or maybe the office was like a dungeon—dark, damp, and full of spider webs. Or maybe—

"Come on, Joe," said Mr. Trevor. "We need to talk."

To Joe's surprise, the principal's office was a bright room. There were colorful paintings and posters on the walls. Behind the principal's desk was a globe of the world. A gumball machine sat nearby. And a small sign on the desk read, "World's Greatest Dad."

As he sat down, Joe glanced at a photo near the sign. Judging by the bushy eyebrows and dark eyes of the young people in the picture, they were related to Mr. Trevor.

"Well, well, well, Joe B. Gray. This is highly irregular. I certainly never expected to see *you* in here for something like this."

Joe opened his mouth to speak, then decided it might be better to listen.

"I'm rather familiar with your older brothers," said Mr. Trevor, as he flipped through a file. "Let's see, George was caught littering on school property. Neil made quite a ruckus in the school library. Henry was caught chasing someone through the halls. Paul put gum on a classmate's chair. And Wayne . . . well, let's just say Wayne was a regular visitor. But you, Joe, have never caused any trouble at all. Your conduct has been perfect. So what happened?"

Where could Joe possibly begin? "Well, Mr. Trevor, it's kind of hard to explain—"

"Hard to explain? I heard you took a frog on the bus, Joe. And that you let it leap all over. That you frightened the kids and threatened their safety!"

"Not exactly, sir," said Joe.

"Not exactly? Did it leap all over the school bus?"

"Yes."

"Did it frighten the kids?"

"Yes."

"Did it threaten their safety?"

"Yes. Sort of."

"So what *didn't* exactly happen with this frog?"

"Well," said Joe, "it was actually a toad."

For a second, Mr. Trevor's lips twitched, then

he gazed down at his desk. When he looked up again, his mouth was set in a stern line.

"Joe, I know it isn't always easy being a kid. Heck, I was once a kid myself," Mr. Trevor said. He went on, sounding as if this were a memorized speech—one he had given many times before. "I know that you don't always think it's fair that you're forced to go to school for hours every day. I know that you'd rather be out riding a bike or building a fort or trading baseball cards or having a snowball fight. Do they still have snowball fights? They did in my day . . . ."

Joe tried to listen. He really did. But it was hard to concentrate because a thought had crept into his head. It was a thought so terrifying, so horrifying, so petrifying that it made his head hurt: Where was Freddy?

"I know it doesn't seem right that your parents go to work every day and get paid. But you work just as hard and you don't make a dime," Mr. Trevor continued. "If you're lucky, you get an allowance, but you're still not allowed to do much. Am I right?"

Joe nodded, but his mind wasn't on what Mr. Trevor was saying. He stole a glance under the principal's desk. No sign of Freddy there. He peeked at the bookshelves lining one wall. No

Freddy there, either. He turned his head slightly to check his shoulders. First one . . . nope. Then the other . . . nope again.

Mr. Trevor was still talking. "But being a kid can also be a magical time. It's when your brain is like a sponge. You can fill it with all kinds of fascinating facts. Facts that, trust me, will be useful and important when you're an adult. That's what school is for."

Just then Joe caught a glimpse of something. He saw . . . oh no! . . . a purple beard and an orange hat. A green jacket and yellow boots. Freddy was standing on top of Mr. Trevor's globe!

This particular globe was one of the fancy ones. It was bumpy in parts, so you could feel the mountains. To Joe, it looked like Freddy was standing about where Mount Everest was located. The little man had his hands raised in triumph, as if he had just scaled the world's highest peak.

Joe knew that Freddy knew that Joe could see him, but the principal couldn't. He knew this by the mischievous gleam in the little man's eyes.

And then Freddy started jogging in place.

"An education can open many doors for you," Mr. Trevor was saying. But his words started to blend together. So all Joe heard was "Blah blah blah yadda yadda yadda blah blah blah." Joe's attention was focused on the miniature man jogging on the principal's globe. Freddy acted like the world was his personal treadmill. The globe began to turn slowly. Then faster and faster and faster.

Mr. Trevor was still talking, of course, so he didn't notice the spinning noise. But Joe did.

"It's school policy blah blah blah blah," said the principal, as Joe gritted his teeth. "Safety is our number one concern yadda yadda yadda," he continued, as Joe gripped the sides of his chair. "We can't have students being blah blah blah blah," he added, as Joe's knuckles turned white.

By now, Freddy's feet were a blur. The globe was spinning so quickly that the little man was out of control. He lost his balance, wobbled for a few seconds, and then fell flat on his face somewhere in the Pacific Ocean. Joe watched as the 8-inch-tall man held on to the Hawaiian Islands for dear life. Meanwhile, the globe spun merrily.

And then something even worse happened: Joe got the urge to giggle.

It's one thing to be lectured by the school principal. It's quite another to laugh in his face while he's giving the lecture. Joe bit his lips. He clenched his fists. He tried to look at Mr. Trevor without looking at Freddy, which was nearly impossible.

"Blah blah blah blah blah," said the principal, as the globe finally slowed and stopped. Freddy rose to his feet with a odd look on his face. The little man staggered. He walked clockwise in circles. Then he walked counterclockwise. He was so dizzy that his feet seemed to have a mind of their own. He leaned to the left. He leaned to the right. He leaned backward and then tumbled forward onto the window ledge.

Joe choked back a laugh as Mr. Trevor kept talking. Freddy kept walking. He nearly fell off the ledge once, twice, three times. But each time, he regained his footing at the last possible moment.

The fourth time, however, Freddy ran out of windowsill. As his right foot felt nothing but air, the little man waved his arms frantically. Then he began a slow fall. Luckily, one of his arms caught hold of something on the way down—the lever on the gumball machine.

So there was Mr. Trevor ("Yadda yadda blah blah blah"), and there was Freddy, hanging by his fingertips onto a gumball machine. And there was Joe, trying his hardest not to burst out laughing.

By this time, Joe's pent-up laughter had reached the stage where some of it *had* to leak out. Still, he held most of it in—until Freddy managed to get his feet up against the surface of the gumball machine.

The little man pushed off with both feet, aiming his body for the principal's desk. He sailed through the air and landed with a muffled kerplunk atop some papers. At the same moment, a laugh burst from Joe's lips. He quickly converted it to a cough.

"Here, take this," said Mr. Trevor. He handed Joe a tissue, which only made him more giggly.

"Now, you've never been in trouble before," the principal was saying. Meanwhile, practically under the man's nose, Freddy wobbled his way across the desk.

"I'm going to give you another chance," Mr.

69

Trevor continued, as Freddy stumbled over a pencil. "However, I don't want to hear about any more frogs—er, toads—on the bus," he said.

Freddy tripped over a stapler and tumbled off the edge of the desk. Joe was trying so hard not to laugh that his throat was burning, his eyes were itching, and his ears were twitching.

"Now get to class before I change my mind," Mr. Trevor said. "You can pick up your frog—er, toad—in the science room after school." The principal finished speaking just as Freddy fell into Joe's lap.

All Joe could do was nod. He couldn't open his mouth to say "I will" or "Thanks" or "Yes, sir" because he was too busy holding his breath.

Joe continued to hold his breath until he made it to the hallway. But then he lost control. Waves of laughter rolled over him. He fell against a locker, slithered to the floor, and grabbed his sides.

"See," said Freddy, "I told you I'd make you smile."

8

The Capital of Florida Is ... Abe Lincoln?

"**W**hy are you doing this to me?" Joe asked, as he made his way to class.

"Doing what?" asked Freddy from his perch on Joe's shoulder. He was trying to look innocent, but it wasn't working.

"You say you're trying to help me, but—"

"Ah, but I'm helping myself, too," Freddy interrupted.

Joe turned to face the man resting on his right shoulder. "You are? How?"

Now Freddy tried to look sad. He took off his orange top hat and squished it in his hands. He attempted to transform his usual toothy grin into a solemn frown.

"You know, it's not easy being the man in charge of the light in the refrigerator," Freddy said. "You're on call at all hours of the day and night. You have no control over how your home is decorated. Do you think I would put the soy sauce next to the salad dressing? Hah! I find that in very poor taste. You also have no control over what's available to eat, though there's always a fine selection to nibble on. Oh, and you're kept up at all hours by the constant noise from the neighbors upstairs."

"Neighbors?" Joe looked bewildered.

"Why, of course. In the freezer."

Joe still seemed confused, so Freddy explained. "You didn't fall for all that talk about a machine called an ice maker, did you? It takes a whole team of little people to collect the water, freeze it into chunks, and chop it up. And trust me, the noise is almost unbearable."

"So why don't you just leave?" Joe asked.

"Oh, that's not allowed," Freddy replied. "I have a very important responsibility. Only the best of the best little people get to be KOFLs."

"KOFLs?"

"Keepers of the Fridge Light," said Joe. "Most of my people have much easier jobs. They live in pencil sharpeners or leaf blowers or player pianos.

In fact, there are only two reasons I ever get to take a break from my refrigerated world. One is the annual KOFL Convention, which isn't fun at all."

"How come?" asked Joe, who was beginning to realize that Mr. Trevor was right. School *was* a place to learn all kinds of fascinating facts.

"Oh, it's a great big bore. Imagine thousands of miniature people just like me . . ."

Joe shuddered at the thought.

"They get together, and all they do is brag about their refrigerators. You know, how they just moved into a double-door model or how their vegetable drawer is the most organized one in the county or how the people they live with put names and dates on the containers of leftovers. But I don't have much to brag about. No offense, kid, but the Gray family refrigerator is *this close* to being a total disaster. So the KOFL Convention is less fun for me than a yawning festival. All in all, I'd rather watch milk curdle."

Joe nodded. "I can understand that," he said. "So what's the other reason you get to take a break?"

Freddy's grin returned full force. "If someone in the family I live with directly asks for my help."

"But I didn't really . . ."

"Come, come! Let's avoid irrelevant details, shall we?" said Freddy. "Just let me enjoy my vacation, okay?"

Joe sighed. Freddy might be having a vacation, but Joe was just having trouble.

They had arrived at Mrs. Tormina's classroom. As Joe reached out to open the door, Freddy pulled an apple out of his jacket. He dropped it into the palm of Joe's hand.

All of Joe's classmates turned to face him as he entered. Mrs. Tormina frowned at him for coming in late. But her frown weakened when she saw the apple.

"Thank you, Joe," she said, taking the apple from him. "Now sit down. We were just discussing all the interesting facts we've learned recently

about colonial America. I want to find out how much information you people have absorbed so far. I'm going to state some random facts. Anyone who knows an answer, raise your hand."

At this, Mrs. Tormina started her usual routine. "The smallest state in the country is . . . Hank Latham."

"Rhode Island," answered Hank Latham.

"Good. Now, Rhode Island was one of the 13 original colonies, but it wasn't the first to become a state. That one was . . . Casey Connors."

"Delaware," said Casey Connors.

"Right. It's the second-smallest state, but it can always boast that it was the first one, too," said Mrs. Tormina. "It became a state in 1787, but the Declaration of Independence was signed several years earlier. The date was July 4, . . . Talia Hahn."

"It was 1776," said Talia Hahn. As always, she kept her hand in the air long after she had answered the question.

"Raise your hand!" whispered a voice in Joe's left ear. Joe reached up and brushed at Freddy as if he were a fly buzzing around his head.

"Come on, Joe, do it," said Freddy as he righted himself. "You know you want to."

Joe ignored the little man. Mrs. Tormina went on with her random statements. By now, about half the students in the class had provided an answer. But not Joe.

"You try to help someone and what do you get?" muttered Freddy. Joe ignored this as well.

The little man moved away from Joe's ear and settled on his shoulder. To Joe's relief, Freddy started to study the room. That will keep him busy, thought Joe. The walls were covered with interesting posters and signs. There were maps of the world and of different countries in it. As far as Joe was concerned, Freddy could spend the rest of the class checking them out.

"The Declaration of Independence," Mrs. Tormina said next, "was primarily written by . . ."

"San Francisco!" shouted Freddy, who had been looking at a map of the U.S. Of course, it was Freddy sounding like Joe.

There were a few giggles, a couple of gasps, and lots of raised eyebrows.

"No, Joe," said Mrs. Tormina with a curious look on her face. "It was signed in Philadelphia, if that's what you mean. But it was primarily written by Thomas Jefferson."

Joe shot Freddy a withering look and slumped a bit in his chair.

"Anyway," said Mrs. Tormina, "Jefferson began by writing, 'We hold these truths to be self-evident: that all men are created . . .'"

"Equator!" shouted Freddy in Joe's voice.

This time, there were more snickers and giggles from the class.

Mrs. Tormina looked at Joe more closely. "I think you mean 'equal,' Joe," she said. "All men are created equal. And by the way, that applies to this classroom, too. So while I appreciate your unexpected participation, I must insist that you raise your hand if you think you know the answer. That's what I expect *all* of you to do."

Joe nodded and slumped even lower.

"Where were we?" Mrs. Tormina went on. "Oh yes, the Declaration of Independence. There were a total of 56 men who signed the Declaration, but one man did it with a much bigger signature than everyone else. He was the first person to sign and later became the Governor of Massachusetts. His name was . . ."

Almost everyone in the class had a hand in the air—including Joe. He knew the answer. He was positive of it. All he had to do was wait and hope Mrs. Tormina called his name.

But that wasn't going to happen. Before Mrs. Tormina could call on Joe or anyone else, a Joe-like voice shouted out a name. A name that appeared on a poster on the wall nearest Joe's desk. A baseball poster.

"Babe Ruth!"

Everyone cracked up. Everyone except two people. One was Joe. The other was Mrs. Tormina. She glared at Joe.

Joe tried to save the situation. "I . . . I'm sorry, Mrs. Tormina. I know the answer. It's John Hancock. It . . . it wasn't me who shouted out Babe Ruth's name."

"Oh?" said Mrs. Tormina. Joe could tell right away that she didn't believe him. "Are you telling me some invisible person just happens to have your voice?"

"Well . . . sort of." Joe had no idea what to say. "It wasn't me. It was Freddy."

"Freddy?" asked Mrs. Tormina in the same disbelieving voice. "There's no Freddy in this class. There's a Frank, a Phil, a Felipe, a Fawn, a Phyliss, and a Flora. But there's no Freddy. First you disrupt my class, and now you're making up stories. I'm very disappointed, Joe. Need I remind you that I've been teaching here since . . ."

"1812!" shouted Joe's voice.

And that's how Joe B. Gray, the boy who never got any attention, set a world record of sorts at Middletown Middle School. Fifteen minutes after leaving the principal's office, he was back again.

9

Goal!

This time, Mr. Trevor didn't give Joe a second chance. "I understand that you're excited about places and names and dates," he said.

Joe, who held Freddy tightly in one hand, said nothing.

"So," continued Mr. Trevor, "you can stay after school today. You can help Mrs. Tormina put up a new batch of maps and posters and signs."

Joe couldn't believe it. But what could he do? Mrs. Tormina wasn't about to believe his story of a little purple-bearded man in an orange hat. So there was certainly no sense in offering the same excuse to the principal. Joe couldn't possibly explain that the man was invisible and silent— except when he used Joe's voice. He couldn't describe how Freddy had latched onto him like, well, like mold latches onto some stale cheese. Teachers and principals had trouble accepting the excuse that "My dog ate my homework." What would they think about blaming things on a little fellow from the fridge?

Today was the first time Joe had ever gotten into any real trouble at school. He had never had to stay after school before. However, George, Neil, Henry, Paul, and Wayne had stayed after so often that Mrs. Gray never expected them to arrive at home on time.

It's funny, actually, thought Joe. Freddy thinks he's helping me get attention, when all I've ended up getting is *de*tention. And that hardly makes me special or different from my brothers. It makes me just like them.

Joe left Mr. Trevor's office and slowly went back to join his class in the gym. He slunk through the hallway, his head hung low, his shoulders drooping. Even the shoulder that held Freddy.

Freddy pulled a pineapple out of his jacket. Joe ignored him.

The little man balanced the pineapple on his nose.

There was no reaction from Joe.

Freddy shimmied down Joe's arm, then his leg. He ran forward a few steps and again balanced the pineapple on his nose.

Joe just shuffled on past.

Freddy ran ahead of Joe. He reached into his jacket one more time and pulled out a lemon, an orange, and a soft-boiled egg. Then he began to juggle these objects while balancing the pineapple on his nose.

Still nothing.

Freddy let everything drop to the floor. He climbed back up to Joe's shoulder. "Listen, Joe," he said. "I can see that today isn't turning out exactly the way you'd hoped. But I'm just doing what you asked me to do. You wanted to be special for a day. You wanted to be noticed. Trust me, you're the most noticed kid in school."

Joe shook his head. "I meant special, as in good. Not special, as in goofy," he said.

Freddy scratched his head, rubbed his beard and then pulled the massive dictionary out again. He began to flip through it, murmuring to himself. "Let's see . . . I don't think you mean special as much as you mean . . . hmmm . . . 'aardvark' . . . 'abdomen' . . . 'absurd' . . . 'accident' . . . Ah, here it is . . . 'admired: to regard with pleasure, wonder, and approval.'"

Freddy slammed the dictionary shut and stuck it back into his jacket. Holding on to the fabric of Joe's shirt, he leaned forward so he could face him. "You want to be admired."

Joe shrugged. "I guess I do."

"Well," said Freddy, as they arrived at the gym, "how hard could that be?"

Mr. Clipowitz had already directed the kids to choose sides for a soccer game. Joe arrived just in time to be added to one team.

It quickly became apparent that this was going to be the typical soccer game. Max Kline was doing a superb job in the goal. Rashaan James was making crisp passes to teammates all over the field. Adam Hanson was booming kicks toward the net. And Joe wasn't touching the ball.

It wasn't that Joe was daydreaming. He wasn't in the mood to receive an unexpected kick in the face. It was just that he spent most of his time keeping an eye on Freddy. The little man had left Joe's shoulder. He was standing silently on the sidelines, stroking his purple beard and watching the game carefully. He's quiet, thought Joe. Too quiet.

When Adam Hanson scored a goal, Freddy watched quietly. Adam's teammates patted him on the back. They high-fived him and told him "Great kick!" and "Good job!" and "Way to go!"

When a player scored a goal for the other team, Freddy watched without moving. The girl received the same admiring responses from the kids on her team.

The score was tied 1 to 1, and a wild kick sent the ball to the middle of the gym. Joe turned to keep an eye on the ball. No one was nearby. And he knew he certainly couldn't get there fast enough.

Then Joe saw an orange, green, yellow, and purple blur racing toward the ball. No one else seemed to notice. Of course not—they couldn't see the blur. It was Freddy.

Joe started to run. In fact, he had never run faster. He had to get to the ball before Freddy did. Joe ran until he felt like his lungs were going to explode.

Freddy beat Joe by more than three feet. He was far too small to kick a soccer ball, so he put his whole body to work. He began to push the ball toward the goal.

The other kids saw the soccer ball moving down the field. They saw Joe running just a few feet behind it. To them, it looked like Joe was dribbling the ball. They had never seen him do it so well.

Freddy kept moving. Joe kept following. The ball kept rolling. Freddy zigged, and Joe zigged with him. Freddy zagged, and Joe zagged, too.

Then a funny thing happened. Joe got the feeling that he had somehow walked right into one of his favorite daydreams. It was as if fantasy had become reality.

Here he was in a soccer game that was all tied up. Joe B. Gray was the focus of everyone's attention. As far as anyone could tell, he was dribbling the ball the length of the gym toward the waiting goalkeeper. The voices of the kids on the other team seemed to fade into the background. But Joe distinctly heard what sounded like excited shouts coming from his teammates.

He didn't have much time to think about anything else. He finally caught up with Freddy near the goal. And that's when the little man stopped pushing the ball. As it kept rolling toward the goal, Freddy veered off and headed for the sidelines. That left two things on Joe's mind—the ball and the goal.

He didn't have time to look at the goalie. He didn't have time to listen to the distant shouts of his teammates. He only had time to plant his left leg, pull back his right leg and—boom!—send the soccer ball screaming toward the goal.

Time seemed to slow down while the ball was in the air. Joe's eyes followed its flight as it soared toward the net.

Mr. Clipowitz's mouth dropped open, as did the mouths of Joe's teammates. Joe knew they were amazed at his skill.

The goalie began to move. He ran to the right. He ran to the left. Then he stopped and watched as the ball came roaring past his feet.

Swoosh! Nothing but net!

Time seemed to speed up again. The shouts of Joe's teammates grew louder. They all rushed up behind him.

Joe expected excited backslaps and happy high-fives. He expected oogles of admiration and adoration and other things that he felt had been missing in his life. As had happened so often in his daydreams, he expected to be cheered as a superstar sportsman, a phantom of fancy footwork, a guru of the games. Instead . . .

"Good job," said Rashaan James, but his tone of voice said otherwise.

"Way to go," gasped Adam Hanson, who seemed to be hyperventilating.

The goalie on Joe's team, Max Kline, didn't say anything. He just stood there with his hands on his hips. He was looking at the soccer ball that had just flown past him into the net—his own net.

Joe Gray had scored his first goal all right—for the other team!

10

The Super Sandwich Taste-Off

*A*merika Baines stood by her chair in the lunchroom. "OK, it's time," she announced in a loud voice. "Is everybody ready?"

Six kids nodded their heads and made their way to a table at the back of the room. Along with Amerika, they were the members of the famous Sandwich Board. There hadn't been a vote or anything. Somehow it had just been decided that these seven people would be the lucky ones. They would be the ones who got to eat other people's special sandwiches for free. They were the official judges of the Super Sandwich Taste-Off.

All the judges sat on one side of the table with

Amerika in the center. Herman Glick was there, rubbing his glasses on his shirt and telling someone a useless fact about whole wheat bread. Suzie O'Malley was there, too. By this time she had recovered from the terrible toad episode on the bus. Her "Suzie Q" hairstyle was all Suzie and Q-zy again.

Joe knew the other kids on the Sandwich Board, too, though he wasn't overly friendly with any of them. Eleanor Brock seemed a bit hyperactive, and her voice matched. She was one of those kids who was always just a little too loud. Joe thought she sounded like a combination of an ambulance siren and a smoke alarm. He wished there was a volume button on Eleanor. And that he had a remote control so he could turn her down.

Rodney Irwin was another judge. He was the Middletown Middle School king of the spitball. Rodney could hit a target from 30 feet away. It was pretty amazing to watch, although too often Joe was Rodney's target. Fortunately, that couldn't happen in school. Rodney had to confine his spitball talents to the playground—when no adults were looking.

Richard Hidalgo was the class clown. He had a knack for imitating other kids' voices, and he did it quite well. There were only two voices he never seemed to try—Eleanor's (because nobody else could possibly talk that loud) and Joe's (because Joe hardly talked at all during school hours).

The last member of the Sandwich Board was Theresa Ross. She was always bragging that she was the great-great-great-great-great-great-great-great granddaughter of Betsy Ross. Then she'd go on to explain unnecessarily that Betsy was the lady who supposedly made the first American flag. Of course, Theresa couldn't sew, but that didn't stop her from boasting.

"We're ready," said Amerika, who had long ago crowned herself Queen of the Sandwich Board. "Who are today's contestants?"

Four kids who had been standing near the Sandwich Board table moved forward with their offerings. Jill Stevens carried a brown lunch bag. Michael Romer had his race car lunch box. Carlota Marley held a blue plastic container. And Dean Chyo carried a large bucket—much like a sand pail, only made of metal. For some reason, Dean always brought his lunch in a bucket.

Jill was first. She opened her bag and said, "Drumroll, please." Then she pulled out her sandwich as if it were a precious diamond or a Mark McGwire rookie baseball card. She handed it to Amerika, who cut it into seven even pieces. Amerika distributed the slices to the rest of the Sandwich Board.

It was typical for the Taste-Off contestant to explain what was in the sandwich only after the judges had each taken a couple of bites. After all, what fun is it to know what you're eating before you eat it? So the judges nibbled and concentrated intently on the taste.

Some nodded their heads and said, "Interesting." A few raised their eyebrows and commented, "Not bad." Some scratched their chins and said, "Hmmm." And as usual, Amerika didn't show any expression at all.

Then Jill made her announcement about the sandwich's ingredients: "It's a fruit and fish special—orange slices and anchovies."

This was followed by a lot of murmuring and grinning. A kid near Joe said, "Anchovies. Ugh." However, the Sandwich Board merely huddled together to discuss and rate the sandwich in secret.

Michael was next. He unlocked his lunch box and handed over his sandwich. Amerika went through the cutting and distributing routine. Then everyone watched the judges chew. When they were done, Michael said, "It's my version of a BLT. But it's a bacon, radish, and potato salad sandwich—a BRP. I like to call it the burp."

Once again, heads nodded. A few kids questioned the idea of radishes in a sandwich. And several people chuckled over the name.

Carlota's sandwich was pretty clever. It wasn't peanut butter and jelly, she explained after the judges had done their tasting.

"It's peanut butter and jello," Carlota said. "Lime jello. With bananas and cherries and strawberries." More nods, more murmurs, more grins.

Joe loved to watch the Taste-Off, even if he never entered himself. So his complete attention was directed toward the Sandwich Board table. He was happy to have something to take his mind off the wrong-way goal he had just scored in gym class. That was probably why he only half-noticed Freddy reaching into the green jacket. The little man pulled out several things, including a full loaf of bread.

Guess he gets hungry, too, thought Joe absently. He ignored Freddy, who was now busily sticking things between two slices of bread.

Meanwhile, it was time for the final contestant of the day. Dean Chyo plopped his bucket on the Sandwich Board table. He reached way down inside and pulled out the biggest sandwich Joe had ever seen. It was the Empire State Building of sandwiches. Joe counted six slices of bread, including the top and bottom slices. It was like a quadruple club sandwich. It would take all day just to finish the thing. Maybe even a week. The sandwich could feed all ten of his brothers. No wonder Dean had brought it to school in a big bucket.

Dean's sandwich got an unusually positive response from the Sandwich Board. This was despite the fact that all seven judges were having a tough time fitting their mouths around their share. The nodding heads nodded a little harder. The raised eyebrows raised a little higher. The "Not bad" became "Very good." The "Hmmm" became "Mmmmm." Amerika even murmured, "An absolutely irresistible combination."

"I call it the Kitchen Sink," Dean explained.

"The Kitchen Sink? Why?" asked Amerika.

"Because I threw everything in there except the kitchen sink," Dean explained. "There's salami and Swiss cheese, smoked ham and sliced turkey, provolone and pepperoni, liverwurst and lettuce, summer sausage and sprouts. Oh, and a dash of salt."

The members of the Sandwich Board huddled together for a few moments, then Amerika stood up and declared, "We have a winner. It's—"

"Hold everything!" There was that voice again. It wasn't Richard Hidalgo imitating Joe because

Richard never did. It was Freddy imitating Joe, something he had been doing far too often lately. "I have a last-minute entry in the Taste-Off," said the little man. Then he whispered, "Stand up!" to Joe. He nodded toward the brown lunch bag that sat in front of Joe.

Joe didn't know what to do. You didn't just shout "Hold everything!" to the Sandwich Board and then do nothing. He had no choice but to obey Freddy's order.

Joe slowly rose to his feet and even more slowly made his way to the Sandwich Board table. The whole way there he could hear kids whispering. After all, this was a surprise. A last-minute entry? By Joe Gray? Everyone knew this was the first time he ever had brought a special sandwich. Everyone was curious to see what it could possibly be.

Including Joe.

He opened his boring brown lunch bag and pulled out a sandwich. It wasn't the usual bologna between two slices of bread. He knew that without even looking at it. No, it had to be whatever Freddy had been making. And Joe had no idea at all what might be in it.

Joe handed the sandwich to Amerika. She was clearly still a little peeved at him for the whole toad episode. "There's not an amphibian in here, is there?" she asked.

The other kids laughed, but the comment just worried Joe. Just how far *would* Freddy go?

It wasn't a particularly big sandwich or a particularly messy one. It looked like an ordinary old sandwich. Then again, the Gray family refrigerator had always looked like any old refrigerator. So maybe this sandwich wasn't exactly what it appeared to be, either.

Amerika carefully cut the sandwich into seven pieces. She kept one and handed the others to Herman, Suzie, Eleanor, Rodney, Richard, and Theresa. Then they each took a bite. As they ate, Joe shot a glance at Freddy. Freddy merely responded with his familiar toothy grin.

Nothing happened for a few seconds. The seven judges chewed and chewed. And then, they swallowed.

Suddenly Joe saw seven sets of eyes grow very big and start to water. He saw seven sets of ears turn beet-red. Seven sets of nostrils flared. And seven tongues flopped out of seven mouths like burnt toast popping out of a toaster.

This time, there were no "Not bads" coming from the Sandwich Board. There were no "Hmmmms." There was just a collective noise that all seven seemed to make at the same time: "Yeeeeeeooooooow!"

Joe didn't understand what was happening.

Amid the shouts and gulps and screams, he turned to Freddy and asked, "What exactly did you put in that sandwich?"

Freddy shrugged. "Just a few odds and ends," he claimed. "Some horseradish and spicy salsa and Tabasco sauce. Plus a little hot mustard, garlic, and oregano. Oh, and just a dash of red pepper."

Joe considered stuffing Freddy into his lunch bag then and there. However, his attention was diverted when Theresa jumped out of her seat. She ran straight to a water fountain on the far side of the lunchroom. She didn't take time to figure out how high the water went before deciding where to place her mouth. She just stuck her whole face in the fountain, as if she were taking— and drinking—a shower.

Back at the Sandwich Board table, Amerika reached for her chocolate milk. She upended the carton and poured every last drop into her mouth. Then she grabbed Rodney's milk and did the same thing with it.

That left Rodney with no drink. So he ripped open a squeeze-packet of vanilla pudding and squirted it into his mouth as if he were putting out a fire on his tonsils.

Eleanor just screamed. Loudly. Very loudly. Joe had always thought it was hard to listen to Eleanor talk. But her scream was like nothing he had ever heard before. It was the kind of noise he imagined he might make if a 6,000-pound elephant stepped on his toe. Or if he fell into a dumpster full of envelopes and got 438 paper cuts. That's what she sounded like.

Meanwhile, Herman was rushing for the bathroom, obviously looking for a water faucet. But he tripped over Suzie's chair. This made Suzie fall into Richard, which made Richard go face first right into a bowl of soup.

Then the situation went from bad to worse. Someone decided to be helpful and toss a carton of milk to Suzie. Unfortunately, the kid's aim was lousy. The milk hit the wall. SPLAT! The carton exploded, spraying everyone nearby with milk.

A kid who had been passing by while balancing a full tray slipped on the wet floor. He caught himself before he fell—but not before he dropped the tray.

The whole area around the Sandwich Board Table was a disaster. Food was everywhere. Milk dripped down the wall. Judges screamed and gagged. It was the biggest mess in the long history of the Middletown Middle School cafeteria.

Then Joe realized something. The one who had started the whole thing—the little man in the green jacket—was nowhere in sight.

Freddy had disappeared.

Where's Freddy?

It took a while for things in the lunchroom to get sorted out. A whole bunch of kids found themselves in trouble. The cafeteria monitor accused a couple of them of trying to start a food fight. Cleaning up the mess was only the beginning of their punishment.

But Joe escaped blame. This was mostly because none of the kids wanted to admit to the teachers that they held a Great Sandwich Taste-Off every day. They figured letting Joe off the hook was a small price to pay for keeping the contest going.

But that didn't mean the rest of Joe's day was pleasant. He had spent the whole morning dealing with unexpected problems. Lunch had been a major disaster. And it felt like the rest of the day would be, too. Actually, it was more than a feeling. Joe *expected* bad things to happen now. He still had his after-school detention to look forward to. And then there was Freddy. The little man was undoubtedly somewhere in the building. And wherever he was, mischief and mayhem wouldn't be far behind.

Joe's mother had an old saying: "Out of sight, out of mind." She meant that you didn't think about something too much if you couldn't see it, if you didn't have a constant reminder. Most of the time, Joe had found this to be true.

But that wasn't the case with Freddy. Even out of sight, Freddy was on Joe's mind. The only good thing was that Freddy would be out of everyone else's sight. After all, Joe was the only one who could see him. Still, he couldn't help wondering what the little man was up to.

Joe went to art class because that's what he had to do. He tried to put the finishing touches on his toothpick sculpture. It was the same toothpick sculpture that his little brothers Orville and Wilbur had almost destroyed with their model airplanes. But Joe had trouble concentrating. The whole time he was working, he expected Freddy to show up and turn the art room into a disaster area.

Joe didn't need to do much dreaming to imagine what Freddy could do. He'd probably jump into the wooden car that Tommy Terwilliger had built and drive it around the room. He'd crash through Joe's sculpture and roar over Flora Ringel's watercolor meadow. Then he'd steer right up the side and into the depths of Ari Taback's papier-mâché volcano.

Or he might dip all Joe's unused toothpicks in glue and start tossing them around the room. They'd stick to Lisa Riley's nose and Sharon Crawford's ear and the strand of hair that always stuck straight up from Paul Dewoskin's head.

Or maybe Freddy would find a black magic marker and draw a mustache on Jessica Burton and a beard on Cleo Robeson and funny glasses on Ms. Fiore, the art teacher.

But none of this happened. Freddy didn't appear.

When Joe returned to Mrs. Tormina's room for his reading class, he still expected Freddy to make a grand entrance. Maybe the little man would skip to the back of the book they were reading and shout out the ending. Or perhaps he'd scale the bookshelf or lean on Volume 1 of the encyclopedia set *(Aardvark–Australia)*. That book would then fall against Volume 2 *(Austria–Bongo)*. There would be a chain reaction of the alphabet with all the books falling like dominoes into a massive heap on the floor.

Or perhaps Freddy would rip all the pages out of one of Mrs. Tormina's favorite books. He'd tear them into tiny strips. Then he'd toss them in the air like confetti. He'd shout "Happy Fourth of July" even though it was the 17th of October. (And he'd use Joe's voice, of course.)

But none of this happened. Freddy didn't appear.

Then it was time for science, the last class of the day. Joe slunk into the room, looking right and left for signs of lime green, orange, banana yellow, and pale purple. Surely, Freddy wouldn't miss a chance to turn Mr. Berg's science class into a catastrophe.

Joe could just imagine what would happen. Freddy would probably hitch a ride in the front pocket of Mr. Berg's long white coat. He'd squeeze the ink from Mr. Berg's fountain pen so it splattered all over the coat. The science teacher would end up looking like a 6-foot-tall Dalmatian.

And Joe could only contemplate with horror what Freddy might do during experiment time. The little man would watch the students create a foaming brew or a new color or a miniature explosion. Then he'd come up with a plan to get attention for Joe. Something that would be spectacular and noisy and probably smoky, too.

Freddy would secretly switch Joe's two safe chemicals with another set of test tubes. One would be marked "Flibohydrawaxoglomide: Do Not Touch." The other would be marked "Combustible: Keep Away from Flibohydra-waxoglomide." Joe would slowly make his way to the front of the classroom. He would pour one chemical, then the other. A

voice that sounded just like his would shout, "Watch out! It's ready to blow!"

That's when Mr. Berg would notice that Joe had just created a deadly dangerous chemical combination. But it would be too late. The kids would rush for the door. They'd push and shove their way into the hallway. Then . . .

Boom! Crash! Hiss!

Terrible seconds would pass before the door slowly creaked open. Smoke would pour out of the room, and Mr. Berg would stumble out with the test tube. His white coat would be covered with green slime. The tips of his messy white hair would be glowing. Steam would be coming out of his ears. He would burp a puff of smoke.

Then the science teacher would point straight at Joe, his finger quivering. "Joe Gray," he would say, in a whisper that was scarier than any shout Joe had ever heard. "It was you!" And "you . . . you . . . you . . .you . . ." would echo through the halls of Middletown Middle School, through the town, through the whole state of Kansas.

But none of it ever happened. Because Freddy never appeared.

Finally, the long day was over. Well, it was over for everyone except Joe. He still had to serve his detention, the first of his life. And if Joe had anything to do about it, it would be his last, too.

He returned to Mrs. Tormina's classroom. Frowning, she told him where to put up the new posters, maps, and signs. "The map of North

America goes there. The drawing about the Civil War goes up here. And put the photo of Albert Einstein over there."

"Oh," she added, "you're going to have a little help today. It looks like one of your classmates got into almost as much trouble this afternoon as you did this morning."

That's when the classroom door opened. An 11-year-old with long brown hair poked her face in. It was Kimberly Simms.

"Hi, Joe," she said, though she looked embarrassed to be there.

Joe expected to blurt out his usual tongue-tied response. The possibilities bounced around his brain. Ki Himberly . . . Bye Himkerly . . . My Klimberhy. But, instead he said,

"Hi, Kimberly."

Mrs. Tormina handed Kimberly a bunch of posters, maps, and signs. "Joe knows where to put them," she told her. "I'm going to check back in 45 minutes. I expect everything to be on the walls by then." And she walked out the door.

Joe relayed Mrs. Tormina's instructions to Kimberly. For a few minutes the two of them worked in silence. But soon Joe couldn't resist any longer.

"Kimberly," he said, "what in the world did you do to get detention?"

Kimberly looked at Joe for a second as if she didn't know how to respond. "Would you believe that I didn't do anything?" she asked.

"Oh yes," Joe replied. "Trust me. I can believe it."

"It was all really strange," Kimberly explained. "This morning was perfectly ordinary. But everything went wrong this afternoon."

Joe nodded. It was a familiar story, even if it did sound like the opposite of his day.

"For instance, I went to music class," Kimberly continued. "We were singing 'Yankee Doodle.' Each of us was supposed to sing a different part. But when it was my turn to sing, well, a different voice came out. The music teacher thought I was messing around, but I swear I wasn't doing a thing. It was almost as if there were an invisible man on my shoulder singing in exactly the wrong key. The voice didn't even sound like mine would have even if I *had* been fooling around. In fact, it sounded a lot like . . . Well, it sounded like *your* voice."

Joe stopped cold, a thumbtack in his hand. No, he thought. It couldn't be . . .

"You know that part of the song where Yankee Doodle Dandy is riding on a pony? Well, that voice added something about sticking some cheese in his hat and calling it macaroni casserole. The music teacher was *not* pleased," said Kimberly.

"And then I was in Mr. Rosenfeld's class for math," she continued. "You know how he has that multiplication table on the wall, the one with all the numbers in order to tell you what times what equals what? Well, he asked me to go up there and straighten out all the numbers. Honestly, that's all I tried to do. But it was as if some invisible hand started switching them all around. By the time Mr. Rosenfeld looked back at me, the chart was a mess. It said that three times three equals 64 and two times four equals 81 and five times five equals nine."

So *that's* where Freddy was all afternoon, Joe thought. Unless there happened to be two refrigerator rascals running around Middletown Middle School on the same day.

"Is that why you got sent here?" he asked Kimberly.

"Not exactly," she replied. "The worst thing happened in gym class. We were playing kickball. I was in center field. The ball was kicked past me, all the way to those bushes at the very end of the playground. I'm telling you the truth when I say that it took me only a few seconds to reach the ball and get it out of the bushes. But by the time I got there, someone—I don't know who—had drawn a face on the ball."

"A face?" asked Joe.

"Mr. Clipowitz's face," said Kimberly.

"Ouch."

Kimberly nodded and shrugged. "So that's why I'm here," she said. "Did you ever have one of those days where everything seemed to go wrong?"

Joe couldn't help smiling. "Did I ever."

12

All's Well That Ends Well

Later, Joe and Kimberly agreed that it was the best after-school punishment either of them had ever received. Of course, it was the *only* after-school punishment either of them had ever received. But they never could have imagined that detention could actually be fun. Sure, they worked hard. They put up all the posters and all the maps and all the signs. But they also talked the whole time. And that was the enjoyable part.

Life is funny sometimes. You can know a person forever without *really* knowing them. Often, you simply haven't had much time to talk. There's always a chore to do or a bus to catch or a phone to answer or a TV show to watch or a book to read or a place to go. People are so busy that they tend to pass each other by without paying much attention. So they end up judging one another based on what they notice as they pass. Things like the way they look or the clothes they wear or the houses they live in. Things that don't tell anything about what the person is like or how he thinks or what her life is like.

Kimberly couldn't believe that Joe had ten brothers, for instance. She was an only child, and she had never met anyone with a family as big as that.

"The eleven of you could be a whole football team or an orchestra or a circus act," she declared.

"You know, I never thought of it that way," said Joe. And for the first time in a long time, he was *glad* he had so many brothers.

On the other hand, Joe was interested in what it was like to be an only child. "Nobody to steal your cereal or hog the television," he said, "or take the attention away."

"You know," said Kimberly, "I never thought of it that way."

Then Joe revealed the truth about his middle name—that the "B" wasn't for Brent or Bill or Bob or Bo. "It's just "B,"" he confessed.

"That's so funny," said Kimberly with a laugh.

Joe didn't mind. It didn't seem like Kimberly was laughing *at* him. It seemed like she was laughing *with* him.

He was sure of that after she made her own

confession. "I have the same problem," she said. "Only it's not a 'B', but an 'O.'"

"Huh?" said Joe.

"My full name is Kimberly O. Simms," she said. "That's all. Sometimes I imagine that it really stands for Olivia or Ophelia or even Oprah. But it's just 'O.'"

"Well, it could be worse," Joe said. "We could each have *both* of our middle names."

"You mean both initials?" said Kimberly. She thought for a moment. Then she *really* started laughing.

As the hour of detention wore on, Joe and Kimberly revealed more and more about themselves.

"I'm afraid of centipedes," said Joe. "I have been ever since my brother Wayne caught one and let it loose in the house."

"Well, I'm afraid of the dark," countered Kimberly. "I have been ever since we had a power failure, and I couldn't find my way out of my bedroom."

Joe went on to admit that he had never—not once—been outside the state of Kansas.

Kimberly said that she had never—not once—stayed up past 1 A.M.

Joe told Kimberly about a time when he was

little. He had tried to flush one end of a rope down the toilet, just to see what would happen.

She admitted that she tried the exact same thing with an extra long licorice whip.

Then Joe confessed to what he considered his greatest fault. "I daydream a lot," he said.

"What do you daydream about?" asked Kimberly as she handed him a thumbtack.

Joe blushed. "Oh, that I'm someone important. Someone brave—or at least noticeable. Like a rock star or a sea captain or a hockey player or a superhero."

Kimberly just stared at him for a moment. Now I've done it, thought Joe. Now she knows I'm a total loser.

But that wasn't the case at all. "It's so weird," said Kimberly. "I never daydream. But boy, do I dream at night. In my dreams, I'm an astronaut or a ballerina or a superstar—or even the first woman president!

"But usually I never get to finish my dreams properly," she added. "I always seem to wake up right when I get to the good part. Does that ever happen to you when you daydream?"

"All the time," Joe laughed. "All the time."

Finally, Joe decided to let Kimberly in on a *real* secret. One that it would be impossible for her—or anyone else, for that matter—to believe.

"What if I was to tell you," he began, "that I met a strange man this morning? A tiny man. And what if I said that he's the reason I got into so much trouble today? And probably why you did, too."

"What do you mean?" asked Kimberly slowly. She wasn't looking directly at Joe now. Her eyes were on the map of Brazil that they had just tacked up on the bulletin board.

Joe wondered if he should just drop the subject. But when he hesitated, Kimberly turned to him with a serious expression on her face. "Tell me what you mean," she said.

The whole story spilled out. Joe described everything that had happened. His before-dawn meeting with Freddy and Wayne's salty cereal. The cream donut in Paul's face and the banana in Henry's tailpipe. The toad, the soccer goal, the disaster sandwich.

By the time he finished, Joe wasn't looking at Kimberly. He was studying the Amazon River intently, wondering if he could wish himself to Brazil. He was sure that at any moment Kimberly would fall to the floor laughing. Either that or call for someone to take him away.

She didn't do either of those things. "You

know, Joe," she said, "any other day, I probably wouldn't have believed you. But after this afternoon, I do."

Kimberly carefully pushed the last thumbtack in the last corner of the last poster. Then she turned to face Joe. "Still, there's one thing I don't understand," she said. "You keep saying you're not special. What makes you think that?"

Joe couldn't think of a good answer.

"Wonderful!" said an all-too-familiar voice—a Joe voice, except that it wasn't coming from Joe. "It looks like my work is done."

And there he was—8 inches tall and sporting a purple beard, a bright orange top hat, a lime green jacket, and boots as yellow as ripe bananas. Freddy was on top of Mrs. Tormina's desk, leaning against the apple Joe had given her.

"Freddy!" cried Joe. Then he turned to Kimberly. "Do you see him? Did you hear him?"

"I heard *you*," said Kimberly. "You said your work was done."

"That wasn't me," protested Joe. "It's him. It's Freddy. He's on top of Mrs. Tormina's desk."

Kimberly's eyes slowly scanned the desk from left to right. Then from top to bottom. "I don't see a thing," she said.

"Maybe he can give me a sign," she suggested.

"Tell him to do something to show me he exists. Not something bad, though. Something useful. Something productive. Something . . . fruitful."

Joe wished that Kimberly had used another word. For, sure enough, Freddy did something extremely fruitful. He picked up the apple and tossed it to Kimberly.

The apple sailed through the air. Kimberly caught it, a look of absolute wonder on her face. "He's real!" she exclaimed.

"Yeah," said Joe. "He's real, all right. And, like I said, I suspect he's the reason for your problems today, too."

Joe looked at the little man sternly. "Freddy, did you spend the afternoon getting Kimberly in trouble?"

"Well, I wouldn't exactly call it trouble," replied Joe's voice. But now Freddy wasn't using his ventriloquist trick. So while the words sounded like Joe was speaking, they actually came from the desk.

"I'd call it helping Kimberly get a little well-deserved attention," said Freddy. "After you made it clear that you didn't appreciate my efforts on your behalf, I went looking for someone else to assist. Kimberly seemed like a good candidate. Honestly—the pair of you! You both need to learn to speak up—speak out—speak freely. Anyway, what did you think about your day?"

Joe stared at Freddy for several seconds. The events of this bizarre and remarkable day flashed before his eyes. He thought of angry brothers, leaping toads, thrown voices, runaway soccer balls, and the biggest mess the Middletown lunch room had ever seen.

Then he thought about detention. And about how having a good conversation with one person you like can be enough to make you feel special.

"I'd say the day was a disaster at the beginning," Joe said to the little man. "And it was a disaster in the middle. But it worked out pretty nicely in the end."

He turned to Kimberly, who was staring at the desk and shaking her head. "Now do you understand what today was all about?"

She nodded, but no words came out.

Freddy shrugged. "It's been a busy day," he said, "and I've accomplished a lot. Now what do you say we go home? Some leftover mashed potatoes have been in your fridge for three weeks now. I've been worrying about them all day. I need to add them to my list of fridge-cleaning demands. You haven't forgotten the list, have you?"

"No," said Joe. "I haven't forgotten."

Then Mrs. Tormina entered the room. "Are you two finished?" she asked. She looked around the room, inspecting their work.

"Very well," she said at last, "you can both go call your parents to pick you up. And I don't ever expect either one of you to get detention again, you hear?"

"We won't," said Kimberly.

"There will never be another day like today, Mrs. Tormina," Joe promised. "Never."

"I sincerely hope not. Now, goodnight, both of you."

Joe and Kimberly said good-bye to Mrs.

Tormina. On his way out of the room, Joe walked close to the teacher's desk.

As Joe went by, Freddy jumped onto his left arm, then scrambled to his usual perch on Joe's shoulder. Joe was relieved. He had no intention of leaving Freddy at school. He didn't want Freddy anywhere near Middletown Middle School ever again.

Before leaving the building, Joe went into the science room to rescue his toad, Terrence. Then he and Kimberly went outside. They stood there, leaning against the brick building in comfortable silence and waiting for their rides. Mr. Gray arrived first.

"Bye, Kimberly," called Joe as he got into the car.

"Bye, Joe. See you tomorrow."

On the way home, Mr. Gray lectured Joe non-stop. He said that he expected more out of Joe. That he had always been such a well-behaved boy. That he never expected him to have detention again.

Joe nodded and said "Hmmm" and apologized more than once. But it was a bit difficult to concentrate on what his father was saying. Freddy was talking into his left ear for the entire trip. He was describing the joys of gelatin, the marvels of mayonnaise, the pleasure of pumpernickel, and the wonders of whipped cream. It was almost as if the little man was excited to return to the refrigerator. As if he had forgotten how much he had wanted a vacation from the place.

As soon as Joe got home, he headed for the fridge. The second he opened the door, Freddy leaped from his shoulder and landed on the top shelf. He threw his arms around the container of cottage cheese. "I'm home!" he cried happily.

Then Freddy looked up at Joe. "Just don't forget my demands," he said. "A clean refrigerator is a happy refrigerator."

"Yeah, I hear you," said Joe.

"And there's one other thing to remember," added Freddy. "If you ever need me, you know where to find me."

Joe raised one eyebrow. Not in this century, he thought. But what he said was, "Let's just say I'm as happy that you're back in the fridge as you are. It's one less thing for me to worry about."

"Joe!" said his mother, "Close that refrigerator door. You're wasting energy."

"Okay, Mom," Joe said. "By the way, this thing needs to get cleaned out."

"Fine," said Mrs. Gray. "That can be your after-dinner job. After the day you had, you deserve some punishment."

Joe knew that he had worries beyond whatever punishment his mother decided to give him. What will Wayne and Paul and Henry do to get even with me for this morning? he wondered.

Joe didn't have long to think about it. A bunch of brothers burst into the kitchen, all complaining about Joe.

"He put salt in his—I mean, my cereal, Ma," said Wayne. "You shouldn't let him have SuperCrackleFrostedFruityPops anymore."

Wayne glared at Joe angrily as he threw his backpack on a chair.

"He got cream filling all over my face," griped Paul. "Some dripped on my favorite shirt. He should have to buy me a new one."

Paul gave Joe a shove as he walked past.

"He stuck a banana in the tailpipe of my car," complained Henry. "I should make him eat the thing for dinner. The banana, I mean."

Henry turned his back on his brother.

"That's enough, boys," said Mrs. Gray. "Your father and I will take care of Joe. You're not his parents."

Thank goodness, thought Joe. Right now, he'd be grateful if his brothers would go back to their normal behavior. If they'd ignore him, as usual.

The three older boys all shuffled out of the kitchen to do chores and homework. But Joe had to stay. Mrs. Gray had something to add to Mr. Gray's lecture. She talked about respecting his teachers and mostly respecting himself.

Then she did what mothers do best. She brushed his hair back off his forehead and said, "You must be hungry, and it'll be a while until dinner. There's plenty of food in the fridge to snack on."

Joe thought for a moment, shook his head, and smiled. "You know," he said, "I think I'll stay out of the fridge for a while. Is it okay if I check to see what's in the freezer?"